EARL OF TEMPEST

THE WICKED EARLS CLUB

ANNABELLE ANDERS

ANNABELLE
ANDERS

EARL OF TEMPEST

A Wicked Earls Club Book
But also
Part of Annabelle Anders'
Regency Cocky Gents Series

CHAPTER 1

"*A*re you sure it's okay for both of us to go in, Clarissa?" Lady Lydia Cockfield, daughter of the Duke of Blackheart, had never in a million years imagined she'd enter such an establishment as the *Wicked Earls' Club*—a *Gentlemen's* club, frequented by *earls*.

And if the name was anything to go by, she could only assume they were *wicked* ones.

Lydia tilted her head back to stare up at the mostly unimpressive building, her arm locked with that of her friend and mentor, the Countess of Baxter.

"You're not afraid to enter vacant warehouses on the docks in East London, but you're reluctant to enter my husband's gentlemen's club?" Clarissa teased, looking extraordinarily pretty despite wearing a plain gown for today's errands. The married countess, not quite a decade older than Lydia, smiled impishly as she pounded on the door a second time.

"Bully for you, Clarissa. As Lord Baxter's wife, you've had years to get used to—" Lydia waved her hand in front of the door and then lowered her voice. "—all of this *wickedness*."

"Not quite eight years." Clarissa sighed and then the heavy door swung open for them, revealing a giant of a man. Although he was dressed impeccably, he was obviously not one of the members. It showed in his bearing, as well as the scars on his bald head and the watchfulness in his eyes.

Upon seeing the countess, he bowed. "My apologies for keeping you waiting, Lady Baxter."

"Not at all, Ben. Lady Lydia and I only just arrived." Clarissa smiled. "We've come to have a word with my husband. Is he busy today?"

"No more than usual. May I take your coats before showing you up?"

Lydia squashed down her nerves as she handed over her coat and scarf. If either of her two older brothers discovered that she'd come here, they would banish her to Crescent Park for the rest of her life.

Thank heavens Blackheart was on holiday with his new wife, and Lucas and Naomi were residing at his estate in Kent, preoccupied with their little family.

When Lady Baxter had written to her at Crescent Park, suggesting Lydia travel to London to volunteer at one of the orphanages she and her husband had founded, Lydia had leapt at the opportunity. It had been precisely what she'd needed to get over... well, to move on with her life.

And as she'd become more aware of the lost childrens' plight, she had not been able to settle for such limited involvement.

Which led her to the Wicked Earl's Club today.

A strand of dark hair had slipped out of her chignon, and she brushed it back.

Not even Lucinda, her twin sister, was here to question any of her decisions.

Dismissing any guilt, and curious now that she was actually inside, Lydia trailed behind Clarissa, awed by the dark wood paneling, the rich and gleaming tables, and the ornate sconces and chandeliers. Contradictory to her expectations, most of the gaming tables were occupied.

Even early in the afternoon, it seemed, gentlemen of the British aristocracy wagered and drank.

A few curious eyes followed her suspiciously at first, but she was quickly forgotten when a scantily clad woman stepped onto the floor bearing a tray of drinks.

What would it be like to be so composed, dressed so provocatively in a room filled with nothing but men?

"She's not a prostitute," Clarissa whispered over her shoulder.

"I didn't think she was!" But Lydia had wondered...

"The men aren't allowed to touch her without permission. If they do, they are given only one warning; after that, their membership is revoked. This is a gentlemen's club, not a brothel."

"So they aren't allowed to be *completely* wicked?" Lydia's question was only half-joking. She'd always heard otherwise but supposed Clarissa likely wouldn't approve of her husband overseeing that sort of establishment.

Recognizing a few of her brother's acquaintances standing at a table with a large spinning wheel, she couldn't help asking in a hushed voice, "Is Blackheart a member?"

Even though he was married now, that didn't mean he hadn't been *wicked* once.

"Members' names are never shared, not even with family—or should I say, especially not with family. To be honest, it's likely the main reasons they pay—anonymity and confidentiality."

"So he is?"

"Be good, Lydia." Clarissa's blue eyes twinkled as she wagged a finger over her shoulder.

So he was. But would he remain a member now that he'd married?

Lydia smothered a grin and slid her hand along the smooth wood of the rail as they climbed a wide carpeted stairway.

Most of her earlier trepidation had vanished. She'd expected the club to be darker somehow, with smoke-filled rooms and garish décor.

Instead, everything was both refined and luxurious. A perfect design, incorporating the masculine simplicity of dark wood with tasteful art on the walls and plush tapestry-like carpet.

And if wealth had a smell, this would be it. Mahogany, expensive cologne, and cigar smoke.

"They pay for more than that," she murmured quietly.

But she was forgetting why they'd come here in the first place. She increased her pace to catch up with Clarissa and… Ben.

With Blackheart away, the only approval she'd needed for this endeavor was from her dear aunt Emma and that had been easily obtained. Even so, she and Clarissa were going to require additional funds to help pay for operations and some of the renovations. She didn't have time to imagine the goings-on behind the closed doors of the Wicked Earls' Club.

"Do you really think Baxter will help? He hardly knows me."

"Oh, but he knows me," Clarissa all but sang. "And since I am your partner in this project, I'm confident he'll offer up a significant donation." She stopped behind their giant guide, who was peering inside a small opening of a particularly ornate door, and Lydia halted behind her.

"I MIGHT CONSIDER INVESTING, Tempest. But I can't speak for Bash or Gold. You have to know that neither is fond of you. Have you never considered trying to be the slightest bit personable?" The Earl of Baxter, a gentleman of not quite forty, known for his charm and charisma, leaned back in his plush leather chair. The two were meeting in Baxter's corner office on the second floor of the club he managed.

Jeremy didn't find Baxter's comment at all amusing but brushed it off. Because he had, indeed, come to discuss procuring investors to go in on the purchase of Ludwig Bros. Shipping, and the earl hadn't turned him down outright.

"Doesn't matter if they like me or not, so long as the investment turns a pretty penny." And in the end, when their estates didn't fall into disrepair for lack of funds, they would thank him.

Even if they did consider him an ass.

"It shouldn't matter, no, and yet it does." Baxter leaned forward again to peruse the documentation provided.

Jeremy could practically recite each page from memory. He'd turned every stone before putting this deal together and was determined Ludwig Bros. Shipping would be in his control in a matter of days. He'd have unfettered access to everything: records of past shipments, past customers, and…

Past payments. He would clear his brother's name once and for all.

The fact that he stood to profit significantly from the deal didn't hurt either.

"I suppose—" A knock on the door cut Baxter off.

Without being granted permission, one of Baxter's employees pushed the door open just enough to stick his head inside. "Your wife, here to see you, My Lord, along with another lady."

Baxter had been married nearly a decade, which made it rather embarrassing to see his eyes light up like a lovesick fool. "Send her in, Ben."

Jeremy glanced at his fob watch just as the door opened wide, allowing Lady Baxter, a lovely young blond woman to enter, followed by…

Oh, hell.

Even with her ebony hair tied back in an austere knot, cheeks pink from the cold and wearing clothes that had seen far better days, Lady Lydia Cockfield was more beautiful than ever.

Unresolved emotions ambushed him.

If he'd wanted to meet up with members of the Cock-field family, he'd have lingered at Galewick Manor, his country home in Sussex. Ignoring his instinct to stiffen in his chair, Jeremy remained seated. To do otherwise would imply that he cared one way or another.

The earl rose and moved around his desk, taking both of the countess' hands in his with a welcoming smile. "Clarissa, my love, you're a sight for sore eyes today." For a moment, Jeremy wondered if the man was going to actually kiss his wife in front of him.

"Working hard today, Mason?" The petite lady moved closer to the club owner as Baxter's arm slipped around her waist. In Jeremy's present state of mind, practically nothing annoyed him more than a happily married man.

God might as well open his wounds and rub salt in them.

"I never do." The besotted man obviously wasn't at all annoyed with the interruption.

Feeling almost voyeuristic, Jeremy slid his gaze away from the couple to Lydia, who hovered near the door, her dark lashes fanning out beneath her eyes as she stared down at the floor.

He didn't need to stare into her eyes to know that they were the most brilliant cobalt that existed and felt sucker-punched when she peeked up and caught him watching her. Pink tinged her cheeks before she quickly glanced away.

"Lady Lydia and I are here on business, Mason." Lady

Baxter stepped away from her husband and clasped her hands together primly at her waist.

Baxter turned his attention to his wife's companion. "Hello, My Lady. You are acquainted with Lord Tempest, are you not? But of course, you are. Galewick Manor and Crescent Park border one another."

She nodded. "My brother's and Lord Tempest's estates neighbor one another's. Only a small stream separates their land."

"We're practically related." The words rolled sardonically out of Jeremy's mouth. "Hello, Lydia."

The last time he'd seen her, he'd ordered her to stay away from him. Along with the rest of her backstabbing family.

"My Lord." She flicked her eyes in his direction for only a second, the blue flashing like the hottest fire, before settling them back on Baxter.

"Lady Lydia and I have a proposition for you, darling," Lady Baxter lounged on her husband's desk as she fluttered her eyelashes up at him. "There is a warehouse that begs to be turned into an orphanage."

"Another one?" Baxter cocked a brow, albeit quite enjoying his wife's flirtation.

"As long as there are orphans," she answered.

"And where is this warehouse?"

"Near the docks, at the intersection of Wapping and Tuesday Street," Lydia answered.

"The old fish-packing plant," Jeremy mused. He knew the area well.

It was also dead center of one of the most dangerous districts in all of East London.

Baxter's eyes narrowed. "Please, don't tell me you've been traipsing around alone down there, Clarissa."

"Not traipsing, inspecting. And most definitely not alone. We had Wiggs and Drake in tow."

"Even so..."

"It's quite sound and large enough to house up to three hundred children." Lydia was all business now, not looking nearly as demur as when she'd first entered the gentleman's office. "And what better place to open an orphanage than where most of the orphans are?"

"You mean thieves and pickpockets," Jeremy corrected her.

She pinned her stare on him. "I mean *children*. Some aren't much older than five or six. With workhouses as their only other option, the poor innocents fall victim to the gang bosses. But what if they had another option? An option that would provide them with a safe place to live that wasn't under the thumbs of criminals? And food and shelter? And, depending on their abilities, education? Doesn't everyone stand to gain?"

"How so, My Lady?" Baxter asked.

"If we deprive the gang bosses of cheap labor, they'll have to go elsewhere. That makes for safer offices and docks for the entire district. And less crime means more legal commerce."

In theory, she had the right of it. "Gang bosses don't relinquish their resources easily," Jeremy countered. Having investigated some of the Ludwig Bros. more questionable practices, he knew this all too well.

Crime would always be present on the docks. Battles would always be fought over who controlled commerce.

Lydia lifted that chin of hers and swung her attention back to him. "I'm not naïve, Jer—My Lord. I quite understand that there will be difficulties. But we are here to speak to Lord Baxter, if you don't mind."

"No, no." Baxter rubbed his hands together, looking rather like the cat who'd eaten the canary. "Lord Tempest, here, might be an even better person to help you." The bastard grinned at Jeremy. "Something like this would help attract those investors. Show your more charitable side. Soften your reputation, so to speak. It could be an opportunity to show that you aren't simply a machine who crunches numbers."

"We don't need help purchasing it," Lydia said. "I have funds to do that, myself."

"But we need help financing day-to-day operations," Clarissa explained.

"Until we can attract other benefactors." Lydia appeared quite serious.

"Tempest, what do you say?" Baxter eyed him. "In the meantime, I could meet with Gold and my brother to discuss your little project. Perhaps even a few others."

The club manager had him between a rock and a hard place. If Jeremy didn't have support, purchasing the shipping company could prove more difficult than he'd hoped.

Money to finance operations for an orphanage was a drop in the bucket compared to what Baxter and his friends could bring to the table.

"I'll have my engineers take a look at it," he conceded.

"It's been declared sound." Lydia didn't appear at all happy with this turn of events.

Well, that made two of them.

"By whom? The seller?" Judging by the look on her face, he'd assumed correctly. "I'll check it out myself."

"Perhaps the two of you could discuss the details while you escort Lady Lydia to my wife's carriage. If you both wouldn't mind excusing me a moment, I'd like a private... moment or two with Her Ladyship."

"Not at all." Jeremy crossed to the door, not acknowledging the dark-haired beauty when he passed her. Hell and damnation, even her fragrance still affected him—something sweet but also floral. He opened the door and turned around. "Are you coming, My Lady?" He cocked one brow in her direction, noting her curves were even more voluptuous than they had been before.

She joined him at the door and then tilted her head back, smiling brilliantly. "How could I refuse?"

He hated it when she did that. He narrowed his eyes and frowned. "I don't suppose you can."

CHAPTER 2

*L*ydia's lips trembled when she smiled at him, but she refused to be anything other than professional. She had come here today on business and would not allow her emotions to get the better of her. Even if her knees did, nearly give out on her, when she skirted around him.

He stiffened and scowled, and the part of her heart that had finally started to heal broke open again. Just a hint of his scent, spicy with a hint of cedar, had her remembering other times that they'd walked together.

He assumed she was unhappy because he'd refused to trust her judgment regarding the condition of the warehouse. He assumed she was not happy that she was going to have to work with him, rather than Lord Baxter.

But he was wrong. Her unhappiness came from seeing him this way—dearest Jeremy—hardened and jaded.

Jeremy Gilcrest was an earl, and by nature, had never been an overly demonstrative gentleman, even before his brother's death the year before. He'd been reserved and his smiles had been rare. Duty had always come first. And because of this, many had considered him unfeeling.

But she'd known better.

Jeremy had not been heartless—not with her and not with the people he had cared for.

The fact that he'd shut them out was why she was unhappy. Her throat thickened with emotion at the thought.

"Do your brothers know you are here?" His voice skated over her senses as he trailed behind her. He hadn't offered his arm, and he did not touch his hand to her back protectively.

"Blackheart is on the Continent, and Lucas is in Kent. Aunt Emma has taken up residence at Heart Place in Blackheart's absence as my guardian." She straightened her back. "But I'm not a child."

"Ah, yes. Dear Aunt Millicent. She's the deaf one, is she not? The one who wears obnoxiously thick spectacles."

"She is a little hard of hearing but I'd hardly call her deaf. When did you become so cruel?" Lydia refused to look at him.

"You are not yet nine and ten, and Blackheart abandons you in London to fend for yourself? What on earth is he thinking?"

On her eighteenth birthday, less than ten months before, even though Jeremy had been in mourning for his brother, he'd taken her for a romantic stroll through the meadow that stretched between Galewick Manor and Crescent Park. He'd gently tucked her hand in the crook of his arm and the two of them had strolled to the water-fall at the tip of both estates.

He'd told her the bluebells reminded him of the color of her eyes. And he'd kissed her.

The gentle pressure of his lips on hers had sent her heart racing. The feel of his arms pulling her close had made her blood flow hot.

Now, he acted as though they were strangers.

"I did not expect to see you here," she informed him.

"Oh, really?"

Lydia clenched her jaw.

Four months before, he'd specifically asked her to keep away from him. Against her heart's desire, she had honored that request.

Wednesday, November Fourth.

She'd awoken believing it would be the happiest day of her life, but by the time the sun had set, was left nursing a broken heart. She would never forget the date. It was imprinted on her soul.

He'd presented himself at Crescent Park in the morning and then disappeared into the study with both of her brothers. He had come to ask for her hand and although a marriage between the two of them would be a benefit to both estates, it was also going to be a love match.

Such an alliance would have been a celebrated one—the daughter of a duke to a neighboring earl.

But there had been no celebration that day.

When he'd emerged from Blackheart's study, Jeremy had not come to her in the drawing room, dropped onto one knee, and declared his undying love.

He had marched angrily past the drawing room, slammed the front door closed behind him, and then ridden off on his horse as though the hounds of hell had been chasing him.

Her brothers told her the meeting had not concerned her and then refused to give her any other explanation. None of it made sense, and so—even though it was snowing—she'd donned her half-boots, woolen coat, mittens, and scarf and traversed the well-worn path to Galewick Manor. What could her brothers possibly have done to offend him?

She had been concerned but not overly so. It had to have been a simple misunderstanding. She could fix this. She would talk with him, apologize for her brothers, and he could continue courting her.

She'd entered the library at Galewick Manor feeling hopeful, but that hope had faltered when he'd greeted her with cold and unwelcoming eyes. She'd seen him tired and hurt and filled with despair, but she'd never seen him angry.

He'd ordered her to cease her visits. He didn't want to have anything to do her family ever again. And that had included her.

She'd begged him to tell her why, to make her understand, but just like her brothers, he'd failed to give her the reason why.

By the time she'd trudged home, her hope had died.

Four months had passed since he'd broken her heart. She hadn't laid eyes on him again until today.

But for the murmuring of masculine voices from below and an occasional cheer, the two of them approached the staircase in silence. Three ladies now circulated amongst the gentlemen in the gaming area below, all of them scantily dressed in identical gowns.

From her vantage point, Lydia noticed feathers tucked into their chic but messy buns, their curled hair twisted into tall styles atop their heads.

Trailing her hand along the smooth railing, she felt unusually plain and drab as she descended to the main floor.

"Not all ladies are daughters of a duke," Jeremy chastised, apparently misreading her lingering gaze. He gripped her elbow in case she needed steadying as they began their descent, his disdain somehow palpable even in his touch.

Lydia fidgeted with her gloves when they finally arrived at the club entrance, spotting the same large man from before.

"Mr.... Ben? Would you please have Lady Baxter's carriage brought around?" she asked primly, aware that Jeremy was watching her, leaning casually against one of the large columns that flanked the door.

She hated that she was wearing one of the plainest gowns she owned—a brown muslin, patches on the skirt and unadorned by any embroidery or lace. She and Clarissa had both agreed it would be best not to stand out when they visited the docks.

She also hated that she wanted his good opinion and that the skin where he'd touched her still tingled.

"I won't hold you to Lord Baxter's suggestion. I'll find another sponsor." It might delay the opening of the orphanage, but as Blackheart's sister, she wasn't without connections.

"I'm afraid the decision isn't mine to make." He continued staring at her, unsmiling.

"But if you are involved, you'll have no choice but to work with me, perhaps daily at times. And quite possibly my brothers as well. I thought you never wanted to see us Cockfields again."

"Some things are worth the trouble." He pushed away from the wall.

"You mean this other project Lord Baxter mentioned?"

His mouth remained set and hard. "Yes."

Was that all she was to him now? *Trouble?*

Lydia rolled her lips together, wanting to ask what he'd been doing these past four months, wanting to breach this gulf between them. But also stinging from the animosity rolling off of him.

He'd once welcomed her questions. He'd once allowed her to comfort him. "How is your mother? Is she here in London?" she asked instead.

Pain flashed across his face. She only recognized it because she'd seen it so many times in the past.

"She is here but she is… recovering. She had apoplexy on boxing day." His voice sounded unemotional and flat.

Lydia's hand flew up to her chest. "I am so sorry. I would have visited her if—"

"She's not taking visitors." He refused to meet her gaze now, choosing instead to stare at the gaming tables. "Don't come here again. This isn't a place for ladies."

"Oh." That must mean he spent a good deal of his

ANNABELLE ANDERS

time here then. Did he flirt with the ladies when he gambled? "I didn't know you were a member."

"The club's membership is private." The ice in his voice slashed through to the core of her bones. The look in his eyes informed her that his personal life would be kept private as well.

From her.

She hugged her arms in front of her, rubbing the spot where he'd touched her elbow.

Very well. She refocused.

"If I'm going to finalize the purchase of the Tuesday Warehouse, I'll need your answer soon, before the owner begins entertaining other offers." If they were going to have to work together, she could at least move things along. Not because she didn't want to know him again, but because he obviously didn't want to know her.

If only she knew why!

"Your coat, My Lady." Ben reappeared with the pea-green woolen cloak he'd taken earlier and, at the sound of a carriage outside, disappeared out the door. Holding the garment, she again wished she'd worn something prettier that day, and then immediately squashed the thought.

"Is shabby and ill-fitting the new style, then?" Jeremy asked, watching her struggle to find the openings to the sleeves. "Not your color at all."

His behavior was not only boorish but outright rude!

"We dress this way for the docks. I wouldn't normally —" The coat slipped away from her for the third time, and she all but growled. "Have you lost all sense of propriety? A little assistance would be appreciated!" It was his fault, of course, for making her feel so clumsy.

"What good is propriety?" He all but mocked the notion.

Lydia's heart cracked. Was he so unhappy that he didn't care about *anything*?

"You once thought it was something that mattered." She tilted her head back in frustration, allowing the coat to hang to the floor, her left arm in the sleeve, her right arm free.

"I once thought a good many things mattered." Despite his words, he reached out and lifted her coat for her anyway.

Even through her coat and clothing, his touch affected her. Concentrating on her buttons, she took a step away from him and tried to recenter herself again.

"Why an orphanage, Lydia?" he asked. "Why not leave something so... *impossible* up to one of the dowagers? I'd think organizing charity events would be more suitable for you."

"Charity events?" she huffed. "And opening an orphanage isn't impossible!"

"For god's sake. You're not up to something like this. It's a massive undertaking."

"Someone has to do it. If not us, then who? I never realized before how many children were without homes. *There are thousands of them!* After meeting Clarissa last spring, and then volunteering at one of her orphanages over the holiday, I..."

But his brandy-colored eyes looked cold and bored.

She glared. "You wouldn't understand. Why did you ask if you didn't care to know the answer?"

"Just making conversation. I thought you wanted me to respect your all-important proprieties." His mouth twitched, as though he'd tasted something bitter. "Regardless, you're too young to take this on, and when you get tired of it and the varnish on your pet project fades, you'll likely do more harm than good."

"I'm not the fickle one." She lifted her chin. "Once I begin something, I follow through with it."

"In that case, perhaps you ought to reconsider your decision now. Best to get out early rather than after you're in over your head."

Lydia stared. Was that why he'd ended things between the two of them? Had he wanted out before things went too far?

But it was not. His reason had had something to do with the death of his brother. The thought reminded her of all that he'd been through over the past year.

"Is she expected to recover—your mother, I mean?" Lady Tempest had always seemed rigid, demanding, and even less demonstrative than Jeremy, but with both his father and brother gone, she was all he had left.

"I don't know." He shoved his hands into his pockets. "Where the devil is that carriage?"

He was anxious to be away from her.

Lucky for both of them, Clarissa and Lord Baxter had begun descending the staircase and would soon be joining them. Lydia forced a smile. "If you'll let me know what you've decided after you've had your engineers go in, I'd rather not wait any longer than necessary to have your answer."

"Tomorrow. You and Lady Baxter are welcome to meet me at the warehouse at noon."

Ben's voice, and presumably the driver's, carried inside as the other couple joined them.

"Is everything settled?" Clarissa asked, sliding her gloves on and glancing between the two of them curiously.

"As settled as it can be without knowing if termites have eroded the damn thing," Jeremy answered grimly.

"Ladies are present, Tempest." Clarissa's handsome husband shot a scowl in Jeremy's direction.

"Pardon me. The *dashed* thing."

"Yes." Lydia bit her lip. What could have possibly occurred for him to change his opinion of her family so drastically, to change his opinion of her? Perhaps meeting him here today was fate. "We should know more tomorrow. Are you ready, Clarissa?"

Jeremy was going to have to talk with her eventually. And this time, she wouldn't give up until he gave her some answers.

Because, truth be told, *nothing* was settled.

"Has Lord Tempest always been so... cynical?" Clarissa asked as their driver pulled the carriage into the road. The two ladies were seated beside one another, facing front. Clarissa's hair was not as pristine as it had been when they'd first arrived, and a few of her buttons were askew, but as the two of them were finished with their errands for the day, Lydia refrained from commenting.

"He's never been overly friendly, I'll admit. But he changed last year, especially in November... What with the circumstances surrounding his brother's death... and Naomi and Baby Amelia and my brother Lucas..." Lydia exhaled a weighty breath.

"Lord Lucas married his brother's widow, and is now raising the man's daughter. Oh, but the child is Tempest's niece. How could I forget that?" Clarissa winced. "And Mason had to go and insist Tempest take part in this Tuesday Warehouse project! I know he thought he was doing what was best, but if I ask him, he can fix this."

"Jeremy minds more than I do." Lydia met her friend's concerned look with a weak smile.

"Ah..." Clarissa studied her closely. "I take it he has hard feelings, then?"

That was putting it mildly. "I thought he was handling it well enough, last summer. He even attended their wedding. I thought..." Unexpected tears pricked the back of her eyes. "I thought that he and I..."

"Oh, Lydia." Clarissa stared back at her, horrified. "Tell me you're not in love with him?"

"I'm not!" Lydia shook her head adamantly.

"Oh, but you are. I can see it in your eyes."

Lydia silently cursed her inability to dissemble. Her twin sister, Lucinda, was far better at it. Of course, if she were here, and not with her new husband and his family, Lucinda would see right through her as well.

"Lord Tempest is considerably older than me." Lydia felt the need to defend something that never was and never would be. "Twelve years, actually. But I didn't think age mattered if two people were truly in love."

"It's not his age that's the problem. And you're right, it doesn't matter. Baxter is older than me by nine years. And even if it did, you seem far more mature than most girls your age. You are something of an old soul. But I have a hard time picturing you with him. You are so... optimistic and well-mannered and sweet, and he... is not."

"He used to be—in his own way." She pinched her lips together. "Our families were close, before Lucas and Naomi..."

"But that is hardly your fault."

"I agree, believe me. But he is holding it against all of us." His turnabout simply didn't make sense. He'd attended the wedding; he'd given the couple his blessing. "At least, I think that's what it is."

"What else would it be?"

Lydia shook her head. "I wish I knew." Perhaps it was something she had done—something she'd said. She'd even questioned that she wasn't pretty enough—that he'd decided he wanted to marry someone who was more sophisticated. Only...that was not like him at all.

"One day, he seemed to truly care for me—more than care for me. And he kissed me—twice. And then the next... I might as well have been one of his worst enemies."

"Did he lead you to believe he would make an offer?"

He had. Although he'd not made any promises.

"Perhaps I only saw what I wanted to see. For as long as I can remember, I have been at least a little in love with the dark and mysterious Jeremy Gilcrest. Of all my brothers' friends, he seemed... special. Unlike his younger brother, he wasn't overly boastful, and he didn't joke about ungentlemanly pursuits. My greatest fear growing up was that he would marry some other woman before I was old enough to be taken seriously. In the end, I suppose, it didn't matter."

"Sometimes," Clarissa tilted her head, "these things simply need to work themselves out. I went six years without knowing where Mason was. I didn't know if he was alive or dead—I didn't even know his true identity! And then... there he was." She smiled dreamily and then shrugged. "And the rest is history."

Lydia couldn't help but smile, knowing how happy her friend was. Even if she was a little jealous.

Clarissa tapped her gloved finger to her chin thoughtfully. "If a tragic event changed him, perhaps the opposite could change him back."

Lydia pictured a scenario where Jeremy became very involved with the building and opening of the orphanage. A scenario where he changed children's lives for the better. "Do you suppose that is what Lord Baxter was hoping for?"

"It didn't occur to me before, but it seems like something he'd do. Perhaps your Lord Tempest merely needs a nudge in the right direction?"

Or perhaps he needed a weighty shove.

"I don't want to get my hopes up." Lydia rubbed her chest. The ache in her heart had just begun to dull.

"It can't hurt, can it?" Clarissa asked.

"I'm not so sure about that." She sent the other

woman a weak smile. Even if Jeremy didn't find hope again, at least she would have a chance to learn the truth. And then, perhaps she could move on, putting her love for him to rest once and for all.

"If you don't try now, you'll always wonder. Whereas, if you at least try, even if you fail, you'll know you did everything you could."

Clarissa was right. Perhaps Lydia needed to consider these circumstances an opportunity—a chance to help Jeremy find hope again.

And furthermore, she wasn't ready to give up on love quite yet.

With determination chasing away her doubts, she met Clarissa's gaze. "He's meeting us at the warehouse tomorrow at noon. If he agrees, he won't be free to walk away from his commitment as easily as he walked away from me before."

"Not if Baxter has anything to say about it," Clarissa mused. "And regardless, you and I are going to improve the lives of hundreds of children. How can anyone turn their back on something so worthwhile?"

But Lydia had never seen anyone's eyes look as cold as Jeremy's did today.

"It's a beginning, anyhow," Clarissa added and Lydia nodded.

Or it could be the end. The proverbial nail in the coffin of what might have been.

CHAPTER 3

The next morning, Jeremy planted his cane on the road, sounding an even thumping rhythm as he neared the entrance of the Tuesday Warehouse, located on the corner of Tuesday and Wapping. Since his own office was located nearby, he'd decided to cover the distance to the warehouse on foot and instructed his driver to pick him up here at noon—he glanced down at his fob watch—in one hour's time.

A few urchins dashed past him and ducked into an alleyway, likely looking for trouble. He twisted his mouth into a wry grimace. He supposed these were precisely the sort of residents Lydia wanted for her orphanage.

With the engineer's report tucked safely in his jacket pocket, he was tempted to tell her the structure wasn't sound. She had no business taking on such a project anyhow—saving thieving orphans, for shite's sake.

She was naught much more than a child herself.

If he kept telling himself that, he just might believe it.

A dark figure pacing up ahead caught his eye, and when he recognized her graceful profile, a drumbeat pounded in his head.

What in the hell was she doing loitering outside on her own? At the docks, the section crawling with the worst vermin humanity had to offer?

She turned her head and waved, looking… so Lydia-like.

Seeing her again… it was too much. He set his jaw and increased his pace, refusing to soften just because he would be in the presence of sunshine and light.

He had no option but to work with her… to ensure this little venture was a successful one.

He'd been given no choice but to step in like some sort of hero. Jeremy shook his head. That wasn't why he was here. That wasn't why he was doing any of this.

Fucking Baxton. He glanced up and down the street, looking for earl's conveyance, and seeing none, cursed under his breath when Lydia turned to offer him one of those damn smiles.

"Tell me you aren't here alone." His gaze roved down her lush figure.

She could wear one of her maid's gowns, rub dirt on her face, and go barefoot, for all he cared, but Lydia Cockfield did not belong anywhere near White Chapel.

"My driver is around the corner, so I'm not really alone. Lady Baxton sent word this morning that Little Alex wasn't feeling well, so they won't be coming. And since I didn't want to put this off…" She shrugged. "The door's open. Have you heard back from your engineers yet?"

Jeremy clenched his fists together, tempted to tell Baxton precisely where he could shove any other reputation-repairing *suggestions* he might offer in the future. If the numbers weren't good enough for his potential investors then...

He sighed.

Because he needed the investors.

"I have." He stepped toward the warehouse, and the door opened outward with a scraping sound. The scent of the docks—tar, whale blubber, and... something that distinctly resembled decades of perspiration—hung even heavier inside than it had on the street.

"And...?" She skipped along beside him.

"No major issues."

She didn't appear surprised, nor did she smirk victoriously as she entered the building. He'd known she wouldn't—not unless he goaded her. As long as he'd known Lydia, she'd been sweet, kind, and exhibited perfect manners.

Hell, she'd practically been raised to be a countess—his, to be specific.

It hadn't been discussed openly, especially after the fire that swept through Heart Place, killing her parents when Lydia and her twin were only four and leaving Blackheart to take over the dukedom.

It wasn't long after the fire that his own father passed.

But before that, there had been an unspoken understanding between their parents that he'd marry the oldest twin. He could have dispelled it, but, as Lydia had grown from a child into a young woman, he'd become more and more fond of the idea.

He swallowed hard, disgusted with himself for missing the friendships they'd all formed in the wake of their personal tragedies.

Friendships that were nothing more than ashes now.

Jeremy stared up at the ceiling, some thirty feet up, and then swept his gaze around the empty warehouse. Fluttering sounds had him noticing the white droppings on the floor. Of course, her orphanage was already filling up with all manner of feathered friends.

Wonderful.

"The open space allows for all sorts of possibilities."

Her enthusiasm was unmistakable in how she all but danced into the empty area. Watching her, bittersweet longing crept over him—the memory of watching her dance under other circumstances. At one of the village country dances, and then later, with her brother at her come out.

Jeremy had been unable to request a dance for himself, as he'd already been in mourning. But she'd known he'd been watching, and she'd caught his eye as she twirled around and sent him a dazzling smile.

He shouldn't have attended at all but he hadn't been able to help himself. *Because she asked me to be there.*

"The kitchen will be built in back." She pointed toward a staircase. "Classrooms and sleeping chambers upstairs."

"What do you intend to use this massive area for?"

"Playing." She smiled back at him. "It will be safe, dry, supervised, and when necessary, can be converted for fundraising events. But we'll be able to host garden parties as well. There is an area outside for a vegetable garden, but there must also be flowers."

He cocked an eyebrow at that, and she lifted her chin defiantly.

"Beauty is one of life's necessities. It soothes wounded souls."

For an instant, he saw it through her unjaded eyes. But only for an instant.

"These... children. They have never been taught right from wrong. There will be discipline issues. They will likely rob the orphanage blind and the older ones will bully the younger ones."

He almost felt bad as some of the excitement left her eyes. But it was better this way. Better she did not enter into this venture wearing rose-tinted spectacles.

"You said it yourself," she finally broke the silence. "Some things are worth it."

She was not broken; she was not ready to give up. She appeared to be as determined as ever.

He shoved his hands into his pockets, and then followed her as she strolled across the room, their shoes echoing off the ceiling and walls. "It's dangerous, Lydia."

"I know." She spun around to face him. "I'm well aware, as is Lady Baxter. We have budgeted for security and close supervision—both during the daytime and at night. The children will have proper teachers and a nurse. I can afford the building and much of the renovation. But after that... That's where your money comes in. At least until we can begin hosting art exhibitions and concerts to attract other sponsors."

"So, you won't be draining my coffers indefinitely."

"We will not, unless of course, you cannot bear to walk away from us..." They'd been teasing, but at these words, the spark in her eyes flickered and she bit her bottom lip.

Feeling a twinge of guilt, Jeremy ignored the hurt in her eyes and rocked on his heels. She had obviously done her research. Her expectations appeared to be realistic, and her conviction to seeing this through seemed firm.

She said beauty soothed the soul. Her beauty would soothe any man's soul.

But not mine.

"Baxter sent the terms over yesterday."

She jerked her head up, blue eyes clear and intelligent.

God, he'd missed her.

After spending less than an hour in her company, he was having difficulty summoning the great bitterness he held for her brothers. He'd felt an inkling of it when she'd first stepped into Baxter's office, but today...

All he saw was *her*.

He would help her with her orphanage. Someone had to. It might as well be him. Blackheart was a fool for leaving her with no one but an elderly aunt to keep her in check.

"Have you decided then?" She didn't sound timid. She sounded as though she was presenting him with a brilliant opportunity.

"I'll provide the funds."

~

LYDIA'S first inclination was to bounce on her toes in excitement and clasp her hands together in joy. Her second inclination was to stifle the urge.

But this was Jeremy.

She responded with something in between. "That's marvelous!"

But she did not jump forward and throw her arms around his neck as she'd really like to. And she absolutely did not press her mouth against his.

But this was a step in the right direction.

"On one condition." He folded his arms across his chest, and she could almost believe he was only pretending to glare down at her.

Nonetheless, she tempered her excitement. "And that is?"

"You are never to come here without protection again."

"But I—"

"And your driver does not count."

Surely, he couldn't be serious.

"I'm serious." *Drat!*

He was not mock glaring at her now. This was all out, straightforward glowering.

"I'll have the term added to the contract."

Lydia signed. "That won't be necessary." It was a little thing, really. And once construction was under-way, the building would be buzzing with activity—

around the clock, if she had any say. "I won't come here alone."

She met his gaze in an attempt to convey her sincerity, and his softened.

For a moment, she could almost believe they'd gone back in time. But then—

"Oh!" She ducked and shouted out when a bird swooped down at her from the rafters. It didn't really come close, but...

Jeremy was looking grim again.

"I've seen enough. Once I've studied the plans, I'll do a thorough walkthrough with the project foreman." He grasped her elbow, steering her toward the door.

"We have preliminary plans drawn up. I'm afraid I didn't think to bring them."

"You can send them to my offices by messenger."

"You have offices?" Lydia glanced over at him.

"Did you think I spent all my time pursuing leisure?"

He pushed the door open, and they stepped outside again. Without fail, the scent of the docks energized her. "You are dabbling in commerce?" It made sense, really. Although quiet and watchful, he'd always kept himself busy.

He was a good deal like Blackheart in that way. Only without the bossiness of her brother.

"I'm purchasing a shipping company—Ludwig Bros." Rather than showing any sort of excitement, his eyes narrowed and his jaw tightened.

"And this is why Lord Baxter insisted you help me? You need to convince some of his wealthy friends to invest?"

He turned her in the direction where her driver ought to be waiting. "Perhaps."

Lydia walked silently. She'd heard of Ludwig Shipping before. She'd overheard Lucas and Blackheart discussing it. A shiver ran through her, and Jeremy pulled her closer.

He could act the uncaring rogue all he liked, but when push came to shove, he would always be a gentleman.

The street came into view, and she frowned. "Coachman John said he'd wait right here."

Jeremy pursed his lips and then gave her an admonishing look.

"I've no doubt he'll return shortly," she added.

If either of them had been paying attention to their surroundings, Lydia might have been able to defend herself against the small boy who appeared from nowhere and slammed into her legs.

Jeremy prevented her from losing her balance, but she dropped her reticule.

"Pardon me," she began. The poor child was collecting her belongings for her, but when she reached out for them, he spun around, and from what she could tell, had all intentions of dashing off with it.

And he would have succeeded if Jeremy wasn't so agile.

The boy was skin and bones, his trousers too small, his shirt filthy, and his jacket at least three sizes too large.

Her grim-looking companion dangled the poor thing by his collar.

"Going somewhere?" He lowered the child so his feet

touched the pavement again but didn't loosen his hold. "I believe you have something that belongs to this lady."

The boy squirmed. He couldn't be much older than five or six and looked as though he hadn't eaten a full meal in weeks. He had full lips and a face that resembled those in paintings. But his eyes... they were a violet color, almost too large for his face, set wide and fringed with thick, dark lashes.

Rather than childlike innocence, however, suspicion and contempt lurked in them.

"Le' me go, Mister! Your 'urtin' me!" He twisted his little mouth, and a deep scowl etched on his forehead, barely visible behind shaggy black strands of hair.

Lydia couldn't help but notice that his fingernails were overly long and terribly dirty.

"You'll do well to hand over the lady's purse, first."

The child's struggling stopped, and he frowned. "'Ere ya go." He held out her reticule, and Lydia cautiously took it from him.

"And your other hand." Jeremy jerked the boy, who whipped his face around to stare up at him in surprise.

"I don't 'ave nuthin' else—"

Jeremy jerked him again, and the boy turned back, opening his other hand to reveal the small coin purse that had been in her reticule.

Lydia took it but then promptly loosened the strings and opened it. "A reward for finding this for me." She placed a coin into the boy's hand.

"Oh, for God's sake, Lydia!" Jeremy dropped his head back, rolling his eyes. "A *reward*?"

"What's your name, sweetheart?" She ignored him in favor of the boy.

Those violet eyes narrowed. "Wot do ya need wif me name?"

"My name is Lydia. I'm purchasing the Tuesday Warehouse to open an orphanage. I simply wanted to know to whom I might extend a personal invitation."

"I don' loike orphanages."

"But there will be plenty of food for children like you, and toys, and a warm bed. I just thought I'd let you know. There will be dozens of builders fixing it up over the next several weeks. And when it's finished, you are welcome to come take a look. Even before it's finished, if you like. Just ask for me."

"Liddy?"

She laughed. It was close enough. "And your name is...?"

"Me name is Ollie."

"An apology for Lady Lydia, Ollie," Jeremy said.

Lydia could see that Jeremy's hold was beginning to loosen. A gust of very cold wind chose that moment to rush down the street, and even as she longed for the comfort of a warm fire and a hot cup of tea, her heart ached knowing that this child wouldn't have either.

"I apologize, M' Lydy." Ollie shivered, and Lydia glanced at Jeremy with a wince.

A carriage pulled up beside them, but it wasn't one of her brother's. "Hold this." Jeremy slid Ollie's collar into her hand. "Don't let him get away." Lydia obeyed even though she did not really believe that the child would run from her.

Jeremy shot a warning glance in Ollie's direction before greeting the driver.

His driver.

Opening the door, he reached inside and went rummaging through the box beneath the bench seat. While trying to see what Jeremy was up to, Lydia clung to Ollie, not because she wanted to imprison him so much as she wasn't willing to watch him disappear into the cold to god only knew where.

When Jeremy emerged, he was holding a bundle of…

Clothing.

"Here, why don't you try this one?"

Lydia loosened her hold as Jeremy assisted the child out of the oversized flimsy jacket he'd been wearing and into a properly sized woolen one. He then promptly wrapped a scarf around Ollie's little neck.

Lydia rolled her lips together, nearly overwhelmed by the urge to cry. Grateful for, and a little stunned by Jeremy's gesture, she watched Ollie scoop his old jacket off the ground and take a step backward.

"No more slamming into ladies, understand?" Jeremy pinned his gaze on the boy, who was looking more than a little surprised by this turn of events.

"Aw wite, mister." And then he bolted, vanishing as quickly as he'd appeared.

Coachman John, driving one of the Blackheart carriages, chose that moment to pull up behind Jeremy's less-pretentious-looking one.

"This is my ride." She gestured, staring up at him, feeling awkward all of a sudden. Jeremy was not a hopeless cause at all.

He glared back at her with cold eyes. "Go home, Lydia," he growled. "And don't come back alone. If I discover otherwise, you won't see a penny of my money."

But she found herself biting back a grin. "Thank you, Jeremy," she said, walking backward toward the second carriage.

"Go home, Lydia."

CHAPTER 4

The following day, Lydia sat across the room from her aunt in the drawing room, staring down at a book but not comprehending any of it. Not for the first time, the memory of Jeremy aiding little Ollie the day before played itself over in her mind.

He had provided immediate warmth to a child in need, and she refused to believe that austerity and indifference were all that remained of his character.

True, he'd not once smiled as he helped the boy into the new coat; he'd been clenching his jaw, and his eyes had been stern the entire time.

But his action had gone beyond charity. Compassion had fueled it. Not that there was anything wrong with donating funds—the orphanage would be quite dependent upon that sort of generosity. But surely, seeing the wonder in Ollie's eyes had to have touched him?

It was terrifying, and perhaps foolish, but she refused to give up on the man she knew he was meant to be. His actions the day before had strengthened her hope.

Hope that he could come to respect her affectionately once again, but more importantly, hope that he would thaw, that he could appreciate that life consisted of so much more than tragedy and loss.

"A visitor for you, My Lady." Mr. Hill stood in the open doorway of her favorite drawing room. "Lord Tempest."

Even though he'd told her he would come, her heart jumped while Aunt Emma merely nodded from where she sat knitting near the window.

"Excellent. Send him up, and could you have Mrs. Duckworth bring some tea?"

They were to discuss the plans, and then later, drive to the warehouse so that she could answer any questions he had.

A shiver of anticipation danced down her spine.

Jeremy appeared in the doorway, the plans she'd sent over rolled up in one hand, and then bowed. "Lady Lydia." He turned to her aunt. "Lady Emma, I hope you are well."

Aunt Emma, who was nearsighted, but not blind, and only partially deaf, held her opera glasses to her eyes. "As well as anyone my age can expect. You've certainly made yourself scarce. Come here, my boy, so I can get a look at you."

Lydia bit back a smile as she watched this proud man bow over her aunt's hand. She was secretly pleased that her aunt treated him no differently than she had all his life.

"You've lost weight. Likely worrying about your mother, no doubt. How is Lady Tempest? Dreadful business, this growing old. And do sit down. My neck's going to get a crick looking up at you like this." Before Jeremy could answer, she turned to Lydia. "Lydia, my dear, you and I will make it a point to visit Lady Tempest later this week. You will find time to come with me in between all this orphanage business of yours."

Lydia nodded but watched to see if Jeremy would provide any more details than he had the day before.

"She is fragile," he said softly as he took a seat on the opposite end of the settee where Lydia sat. Turning toward Lydia's aunt, he leaned forward, resting his elbows on his knees. "She may not recognize you. Most days, she doesn't know me from Adam."

The admission was a startling one. No wonder…

No wonder.

"I'm so sorry, Jeremy." Of course, his aunt would call him by his given name. She'd known him as a child, and then a young man. "I imagine her heart weakened from young Arthur's passing. There is too much tragedy in this world."

If Lydia had not been watching him very closely, she would have missed it. Despair flickered across his face.

His throat worked, as though he was swallowing unwanted emotion. And then his eyes shuttered once again. "We're doing our best to keep her comfortable, for now."

But Lydia realized something that perhaps even he didn't know.

He'd lost the will to hold onto hope.

Aunt Emma nodded. "But I know you did not come to visit me. Feel free to go about your work while I knit."

She glanced down at the two needles and half-finished project on her lap, almost as though she'd forgotten it was there." "If only I could remember what I was working on. Was this the scarf for your sister? Oh, no, I forgot, it's a blanket for the baby."

Lydia met Jeremy's eyes in an unexpected moment of shared amusement.

"Lucinda is expecting later this spring." Her sister had married later in the same Season the twin sisters had made their come out... and then moved away and become quite caught up with her new husband's family.

As she should.

However, it had left an emptiness in Lydia that she never would have expected.

"I remember," he said.

Of course, she'd told him when she'd received Lucinda's letter—when they had shared these sort of details with one another.

Lydia blinked, forcing herself not to dwell on the past. Jeremy was here on business. "What did you think of the plans?"

"I have a few questions." He opened them, spreading them on the low table in front of them, while she placed a candle holder on each of the corners to keep the papers from rolling back onto themselves.

Over the next half an hour, while taking tea, they discussed the design, some issues she'd considered, and some she had not. In that time, both of them had moved to the center of the sofa, and Lydia became acutely aware of his thigh touching hers.

His scent—which reminded her of leather-covered

books, and clove, and freshly cut cedar—only served to heighten her awareness.

She was so in tuned in to his presence that she could almost feel him breathing beside her. Altogether, she was more than a little distracted.

She straightened her spine and focused on what he was actually saying.

"I'm a little concerned about your garden area. If it was used for disposal, you might have problems with the soil…"

"I had not thought of that." Lydia wrinkled her nose. When she'd first toured the warehouse, she'd only spied the yard from a window. Until it could be cleaned up, it was not at all inviting. She and Clarissa had also caught sight of a few vagrants. "I have no idea…"

"No way to find out other than to see for ourselves." He'd turned to stare at her, and their faces were only inches apart. His gaze flicked to her lips, and then quickly back to her eyes. "Shall we drive over now then? Did you wish to change first?"

She barely heard his question over the pounding of her heart. When he'd kissed her last, she had welcomed it, but she hadn't felt like her skin was going to burst into flames the way she felt now.

"Lydia?"

"Oh… oh, yes." She glanced down at her day dress, which would have been perfectly acceptable if she was going anywhere other than the docks. "I suppose I should." She burst off the settee. "I'll only be a moment."

Jeremy only nodded at her. *Had he felt that too?*

Louise, her maid, was waiting inside Lydia's

bedchamber with the plain-looking gown cleaned and pressed. Not quite fifteen minutes later, Lydia reentered the drawing room, pea-green coat draped over her arm.

"I cannot wait for the weather to warm up." She forced her tone to remain light and casual. She could only hope that he was unaware of how he'd affected her. "This winter has been unusually cold. And so much snow!"

As she exited Heart Place, her hand tucked into his arm, she found herself babbling about other ideas she had for the orphanage. It wasn't like her to go on so, and of course, he knew that.

Unfortunately, as she sat down beside him, their proximity in the confines of the coach did nothing to settle her nerves.

"You're excited." His words broke in when she finally took a breath, and her insides trembled.

When she'd discussed her hopes with Clarissa two days before, she'd not taken into consideration what working with him might do to *her*. She was optimistic, yes, but if she lost him again, would she ever be able to fall in love again? She couldn't imagine it.

"I am."

"The Season begins in a little over a month, and construction should be well underway by then. If it's all the same, I'll manage all of this while you flit about with the *ton*."

Flit about?

Flit about?

"What are you talking about?"

"You'll hardly have time for both." He shrugged.

"What? You—" She needed a moment to realized what he was saying. "I'll have you know my priority is the orphanage. And although I plan to attend a few select events and seek out donations." She gritted her teeth. "I have no intentions of allowing the season to distract me. I thought you'd realized this by now."

"Do you not intend to place yourself on the marriage mart, then?"

"I do not." In fact, she'd put all thoughts of marriage from her mind the day after he'd told her to keep away from him.

"You'll change your mind." The arrogance in his voice had her twisting around to confront him.

"Of the two of us." She pointed at him and then herself. "I... *I* am not the fickle one."

He returned her gaze steadily, and she would have given ten years of her life to know what was going on inside his head in that moment.

"Why?" she couldn't help but ask, her voice choking. *Why did you send me away?*

Her question had him looking trapped, and she hated whatever it was that had changed him. He was saved from answering, however, when the carriage came to a halt.

"I have other business to attend to today, so let's get this over with, shall we?" The icy tone of his voice effectively put a halt to her curiosity.

It wasn't often Lydia allowed herself to become angry, but she was sorely tempted to at that moment.

Except they were at the warehouse now, and the orphanage came first.

～

WHY?

He knew exactly what she was asking, but he wasn't about to discuss it with her today. Or ever.

The secret wasn't his to share.

He offered his hand for her to step onto the walk, but she grasped the side of the carriage instead.

He shouldn't be here with her. This situation was untenable. Baxter didn't know what the hell he'd been doing when he suggested Jeremy finance this damned orphanage.

And yet...

Damn his eyes, Jeremy *wanted to be here with her.*

And watching her bustle through the door ahead of him, he admitted that he wanted more than that.

But he could never give her what she wanted: marriage. He could not join their two families together—not while both of her brothers were intent on tarnishing Arthur's memory.

Tarnishing it with the very worse of accusations.

Pushing away the dissonance inside of him, Jeremy watched Lydia shove, and then slam her shoulders into the door, sending it flying open before he could catch up with her and do it himself. She glanced at him over her shoulder, scowling, but not bothering to hide her satisfaction at the insignificant triumph.

Better she release her anger on the door, he supposed, than on him.

Even so. "You'll hurt yourself." He strolled through the opening behind her.

"I'm fine."

She was so *'fine'* in fact, that she spent the next forty-five minutes marching him through the building, answering him as succinctly as possible, and glowering at him whenever she caught his eye. She made it painfully clear that she was determined to refrain from mentioning the past to him again.

All of which he, quite rightly, deserved.

"You should go to the balls and the garden parties," he offered thoughtfully once they'd returned to the ground floor. Even so, he couldn't keep his gaze from settling on her lush hips as she preceded him toward the door leading outside to the vacant land in back.

"Don't be ridiculous," she bit out without looking at him.

"I'll take care of matters here--ensure things are finished properly. You really should land yourself a husband—perhaps a wealthy one who'll happily add his blunt to your pet projects."

She spun around to face him—eyes burning, her lovely cheeks flushed. "This is not a pet project for me!" He'd never seen her looking so worked up before. Not even on the day he'd ended things between the two of them. "What must I do to get that through your thick skull?"

Momentarily stunned, he inexplicably found his heart racing. She was impossible. She was a bloody *Cockfield*, he reminded himself. He forced himself to recall what her brothers had set out to do to Arthur.

"Time will tell." He affected disdain in the face of her enthusiasm.

Because, unfortunately, he already believed her. She was *not* fickle, and even though she was far too young to be so diligent, she would not abandon a worthwhile project after starting it.

"Time?" She was pacing around in a circle now, gesturing wildly with her arms. "Time? How much time do you need? Is knowing me for most of my life not enough to prove my character to you? Or allowing you to hold my hand when we walked alone through the forest? What about the fact that I gave you permission to court me? To kiss me? Is it not—"

Jeremy swept her into his arms. He would silence the reminder of those memories with his mouth.

If she'd pushed him away, he would have released her. If she'd held her lips tightly together, he would not have dipped his tongue behind them.

But no.

She melted against him, like butter on warm bread.

She tasted like the tea they'd drank earlier, that, and the sweetest flower, like comfort and...

Good god in heaven, Lydia Cockfield tasted like *love*.

When he'd kissed her last fall, he'd been cautious, proper. He had not embraced her fully, held her small figure pressed tightly against his.

If he had, he wondered if he'd have had the strength to walk away.

She was as forgiving as an angel. But she was also warm, willing, and sensual. The feel of her breasts crushed against him sent white-hot arousal coursing through his veins. Her soft abdomen absorbed the pressure of his cock, taunting him at how it would feel to slide between her legs.

"Jeremy." She whispered against his lips, making his name sound like a fervent prayer.

Need threatened his self-control. He could remove both their coats and arrange them on the floor. She would be his for the taking.

She stiffened. "What's that sound? I heard something."

She shoved at his chest, her bosom rising and falling with each labored breath. Even though her lips were swollen and shining from their kiss, her eyes were wide.

And then he heard it too. Like a door being thrown open.

And if he hadn't spun around so quickly, he might have missed the sprite dashing through the door.

"Ollie?" Lydia recognized him just as Jeremy wrapped his hand around the child's arm.

A very thin arm.

A very thin and *coatless* arm.

CHAPTER 5

*J*eremy tightened his grip on this urchin for the second time in two days.

"I didn't do anyfin'!" Ollie shouted. "Why you always grabbin' me?" He jerked his arm in a futile attempt to break free.

Jeremy was grateful that the boy had interrupted them before matters had gone too far; however, for the same reason, he was also tempted to throttle him.

Lydia, however, didn't suffer similar conflicting feelings and was already on her knees, running her hands down Ollie's spindly little arms and legs. "What happened to you? Where is your coat?"

Bruises littered those pale arms, and crusted blood mingled with the dirt and grime on the boy's trousers. Looking up into Lydia's eyes, the unruly urchin ceased his fighting and Jeremy relaxed his grip. Rationally, Jeremy knew of the trials these children faced on the docks, but to see the consequences meted out on one so young…

It was a unacceptable.

"You said if I came I'd git help. But no one was here and since I don' have no coins for the boss again, I came here an' hid." Ollie narrowed his eyes at Jeremy. "I wasn' hidin' from you and her."

"Of course, you weren't hiding from me," Lydia all but cooed at the little trespasser. "I'm so sorry. This is all my fault then. I should have been more clear…" She exhaled a guilty sigh. "We need to hire workers first. Who did this to you?"

She was doing her best to remain calm, Jeremy knew, but her voice trembled with emotion. She raised her fingers to Ollie's face and brushed back unruly strands of soot-black hair to reveal a bruise near his eye.

"Buck did. Said it was a lesson I had comin'."

"Buck?" Lydia looked confused, but Jeremy had no doubt that Buck would be one of the older boys in the street gang Ollie ran with.

"I wen' back wi' no' enuf coins for Farley."

Lydia's face fell with the realization. "Oh, Ollie."

"Buck's no problem. But Farley has a pistol."

Jeremy clenched his fists. He couldn't help but wonder if the pistol was one that had been stolen from Ludwig's.

"In that case, you'll simply have to come home with me." Lydia rested on her heels and nodded decisively.

Oh, hell.

"You can't just take a boy home with you!" Good Lord! Blackheart needed to return to London soon before his sister filled not only an orphanage but Heart Place with homeless urchins.

51

"But this is all my fault! I told him we'd be here." She gazed up at him.

"Tha' she did, m'lord," Ollie echoed.

The child would rob her blind.

After spending a few days in the lap of luxury, innocent little Ollie would likely show right back up at the docks with as much of Blackheart's silver as he could carry. He'd break Lydia's tender heart in the process. "It isn't safe, that's why. You know nothing about this boy."

Lydia herself would be vulnerable if Ollie took it upon himself to return to Heart Place with a few of his friends.

"But he is in danger." She stared up at him fiercely, her cobalt eyes unwavering.

"And taking him into your home could place you in danger as well." He pinned his gaze on Ollie. "I imagine Farley isn't very forgiving when he loses an... employee. Am I right, young man?" Jeremy demanded sternly. No way in hell was he allowing Lydia to bring a street urchin home with her.

Ollie squirmed. "I don' suppose he would be."

Jeremy scrubbed a hand down his face. As soon as word got out about the orphanage, this Farley fellow, or some other gang boss, would no doubt start up trouble.

Their control already extended too far, and this just gave Jeremy another reason to neutralize them.

"I'm not leaving him here." Lydia rose to her feet again and crossed her arms in front of her, pushing her bosom up and reminding him of what they'd been doing before being so rudely interrupted.

The housekeeper at his manor on Cork Street was

something of a dragon and ought to be able to keep the boy out of trouble.

Maybe.

He stared down at the orphan, who was feigning innocence all too convincingly. "I might have a position for you."

"You mean you would take him home with you?" Lydia gazed at him with so much delight and wonder that he was tempted to go in search of ten more orphans to welcome into his home.

And at that ridiculous thought, Jeremy clenched his jaw and scowled. "He'll have to earn his keep."

"But you have a warm bed for him, and food, and most importantly, he'll be safe!" The scowl must not have looked stern enough because her ridiculous wonder flourished—in her smile, her voice, and the grateful clasp of her hands. "Did you hear that, Ollie? Lord Tempest is going to take you home with him."

"But I'd rather go with you." Ollie sidled up next to her.

Although doomed to be sorely disappointed, the child had excellent taste.

"You'll come with me, or you'll remain with your friends on the docks." Jeremy supposed he ought to send a watchman over. And repair all the locks. They were lucky the warehouse hadn't already filled up with vagrants.

"You'll not regret it, Ollie." Lydia took hold of the boy's hand and glanced over her shoulder at Jeremy, her full, pink lips tilted up into that devastating smile of hers.

More worshipful wonder.

"We're finished here for the day, are we not?"

Jeremy fisted his hands at his sides. "I suppose so."

AFTER BEING DELIVERED BACK to Heart Place, assured by Jeremy that Ollie would be safely situated in the Tempest household, Lydia lay back and soaked in a long hot bath, feeling acutely aware that but for a colossal stroke of luck, she and Lucinda and her brothers could have ended up just like Ollie. Because she'd been orphaned at the age of four.

Only, her father had been a duke.

Was that why she'd agreed so quickly to work on this project with Clarissa? Because of guilt? She closed her eyes and tilted her head back as Louise carefully poured a pitcher of water, rinsing the soap from Lydia's hair.

Life wasn't fair. Was it wrong that guilt motivated her?

Working out her motivations would have been a good deal easier if her mind didn't persistently return to the most astounding fact that Jeremy had kissed her! And not in the manner he'd kissed her last summer.

This kiss had been... alarming. *Devastating. Exciting.*

This kiss had been magnificent.

Her heart fluttered, and she shivered.

"Your towel, My Lady," Louise assisted her out of the copper tub and helped her to dry off and then don one of her day dresses, a low-waisted jonquil muslin with a V-neck and sleeves large enough to store a small dog in each.

Too discombobulated to join her aunt in her knitting downstairs, Lydia sat down to make notes of what she and Jeremy had discussed.

Only… rather than summon words to write, her mind kept going back to those few moments before Ollie had interrupted them.

Jeremy had kissed her with the same desperation she felt. Did that mean he felt the same?

His lips had been hard and demanding, almost as though he was angry. At her? No, she decided, most definitely not at her.

At himself? Lydia dipped her pen in the jar of ink.

When he'd dragged his mouth along her jaw and then down her neck, he'd softened.

He'd fondled her. *He tasted me.*

It had made her want to taste him as well—to know the essence of his skin in every way imaginable.

Lydia frowned down at the large drop of ink that had plopped onto the parchment and then crumpled it in frustration and tossed it onto the floor.

She'd been exasperated with him one moment and clinging to him desperately the next. Remembering the feel of his body, all hard planes and muscles pressing into her, heat raced to her core.

This was useless. Lydia set down the pen and closed the jar of ink. Had he kissed her because he was regretted sending her away last autumn?

Throwing herself onto her bed, she squeezed her thighs together at the same time she allowed one of her hands to edge over her belly, to just below her breast.

A knock sounded on the door, causing her to sit up guiltily.

"Come in!"

Clarissa peered around the door. "Mr. Hill sent me up." Her friend looked elegant and sophisticated, wearing a puce linen day dress with a low waist and billowing long sleeves. As she entered the room, she removed her bonnet and then tossed it onto the bed.

"How is little Alexander?" Lydia touched her finger-tips to her cheeks, hoping they weren't flushed.

The young countess shrugged and waved a hand through the air. "He's fine. That was just an excuse to leave you and Lord Tempest alone." She dropped into the chair near Lydia's vanity. "Tell me everything."

Lydia shot her friend a disapproving glance but then sighed.

"Well?" Clarissa prompted her.

"He's decided to invest, and he's amenable to the plans we've had drawn up."

"That's not what I mean. Is there hope for him? Did the two of you discuss anything personal? Did he kiss you?"

Lydia bit her lip.

"He kissed you!"

"A thief attacked us on the street." Lydia made an attempt to avoid discussing what had happened between her and Jeremy. Because she didn't quite understand it herself.

"No!"

"He was a child, Clarissa, the most precious boy you've ever seen." Lydia went on to tell her all about

Ollie, and the coat Jeremy gave him, and how he'd returned today, bruised and beaten. And about the gang boss, causing both of them to frown.

"Mason has warned me that there could be trouble. He and Lord Tempest may be forced to deal with the gang bosses early on. But what can we do about the boy until then?"

"Jeremy took Ollie home with him," Lydia announced and then paused abruptly. He'd surprised her. And yet, it was precisely what he'd have done before his brother died.

Clarissa tilted her head in disbelief. "Your Lord Tempest? A gentleman who had to be coerced into the project to begin with? He has opened his home up to an orphan?"

Lydia nodded. "He said his cook would put Ollie to work. And even though he says he's only doing it to keep me from bringing Ollie home with me to Heart Place, I refuse to believe it." She held Clarissa's gaze, almost afraid to appear too hopeful. "I could see it in his eyes, Clarissa. He could no more leave that child alone there than I could."

"But when did this kiss happen?"

Lydia smoothed the fabric of her gown and then shrugged. "Just before Ollie came running in."

"Was it more than just a kiss?" Clarissa asked.

Lydia pinched her lips together, feigning innocence.

And obviously failing.

"Oh, Lydia." The other girl was shaking her head.

Lydia hadn't intended to tell Clarissa anything about it, but since she already knew... "It was glorious. Fantastic. It's never been that way before, and I never wanted it to end."

"Oh, dear." Clarissa looked more concerned than delighted. "I should have thought this through better."

"What?"

"It's a good thing that kiss did end, though. Little Ollie deserves your thanks. You're terribly young and if Tempest ruined you, Baxter would have to send for Blackheart to defend your honor."

Which, all in all, would be an utter catastrophe.

"I really do need more friends who don't read my mind like you do."

"I'm not sure that's possible, what with your emotions written all over your face."

Lydia conceded with a shrug. It was true. "What should I do if he kisses me again?"

"What do you *want* to do?" Clarissa countered.

"Probably something that I oughtn't."

Her friend brushed her hands together decisively. "And for precisely that reason, the two of you cannot be alone together again. At least not until we know his intentions are honorable. I'll host a dinner party next week. That will give him the opportunity to show his affection for you in a socially acceptable manner."

Lydia held back a groan. "Next week?" She didn't *want* to wait until next week to see him again.

"And in the future, I'll not send you alone again to discuss the orphanage with him. I ought to have realized…" Clarissa wagged a finger. "But let him stew a little. He's had a taste, now he must decide: is he prepared to commit to the entire meal?"

Lydia groaned. "I don't know." She wished it was as simple as that.

"Keep yourself busy. Visit Madam Chantal and ask her if she knows of any seamstresses we can hire. The children will need proper clothing and we might as well have them wear uniforms. And if you've time, drop by the employment agency as well. No time like the present to begin interviewing teachers and whatnot, now that we've secured funds." The young countess rose and brushed at her skirts. "I can't stay long. Mason is taking me to the opera this evening. He rather enjoys sitting in the dark with me." A grin flashed across her face, but she schooled it and sent Lydia a warning glance. "Don't do anything foolish."

In the past, Lydia would have laughed outright at such a warning. But on the heels of Arthur's scorching kiss... "I won't."

She walked Clarissa downstairs to the door and then watched her climb into the elegant carriage waiting for her.

What would it be like to... *sit in the dark* with one's husband in a private box at the opera? And to have children of her own?

Feeling lonelier than she had before Clarissa's visit, Lydia closed the door behind her and, after peeking inside the drawing room, wandered the corridors until she located Mr. Hill. "Have you seen my aunt this afternoon?"

"She went out with Lord Beasley one hour ago. She said she wasn't certain of when she intended to return."

Mr. Hill seemed almost apologetic. Lydia must look as pathetic as she felt.

"Thank you, Mr. Hill."

This wasn't the first time her aunt had gone out with Lord Beasley, an elderly baron who'd courted Aunt Emma about a hundred or so years ago. And if Lydia wasn't mistaken, the gentleman was as smitten now as he must have been before.

Lydia needed to stop feeling sorry for herself and do something productive. Just as she went to return to her chamber, however, pounding sounded on the door, fists rather than the knocker. Curious as to who it could be, Lydia paused on the steps and waited for Mr. Hill to open it. When he did so, a gush of wind swept into the foyer, along with Jeremy, who looked fit to be tied.

"Is he here?"

"Who?"

"Our innocent little orphan," Jeremy growled.

Oh, Ollie! Lydia's heart sunk at the implication of Jeremy showing up here looking for him.

"You lost him already?"

"I didn't lose him. Mrs. Crump fed him, found him proper clothing and shoes, and then insisted he bathe, which, by the way, had the entire household suffering his caterwauling for nearly half an hour. But when she sent him to collect coal from the cellar, he disappeared instead."

"Oh, no."

"I thought he might have come here. He paid very close attention to our directions after we delivered you yesterday." Jeremy rubbed the back of his neck. And in that single motion, Lydia saw it. He was concerned that Ollie had returned to the docks and put himself in danger.

Worry swept through her at the thought.

"We need to find him," she said. "We need to go back to the warehouse now." She glanced down at her gown, which would stand out like a sore thumb amongst the fishmongers, beggars, and seaman ever-present along Wapping Street.

Jeremy shook his head. "It's getting late. Perhaps Baxter—"

"Pardon me, My Lord, My Lady." Lydia turned around to see Mrs. Duckworth, the housekeeper, hovering at the door that led to the kitchens. "This little one insists that he knows you."

Tucked behind the housekeeper's skirts, wearing perfectly fitted short pants, a shining pair of boots, and a pristine white shirt beneath a fitted jacket, hid a small boy who looked suspiciously familiar.

"Ollie!" Lydia gasped. Absent his usual dirt and grime, her little orphan was barely recognizable. Lydia rushed forward and took both his hands in hers and then lifted them out to his sides in admiration. "Just look at you!"

"Ahem." Jeremy stepped forward with a scowl, and Ollie's relieved smile fell.

"Tell me, Oliver, did or did not Mrs. Crump ask you to bring up some coal." Jeremy pointedly swept his gaze around the gilded foyer. "You are a long way from my coal cellar. Did you get lost?"

Lydia bit her lip and watched silently. This was a matter to be settled between the two of them.

Ollie squirmed. "I don't like no baths. That old woman dumped hot water over my head—tried to drown me." And then he threw his arms around Lydia's legs. "Don't make me go back!"

Lydia pinched her mouth into a straight line and stared at Jeremy expectantly, all but biting her tongue so as not to interfere.

Hands behind his back, Jeremy stood firm, looking quite imposing but also... like that of a disappointed parent.

"You promised me you would assist in the kitchen, and in exchange, what did I promise you in return?

"Hot food. And sweet biscuits, and a bed that ain't outside," Ollie admitted grudgingly.

"And what did you have when we arrived at Charles Street?"

"Stew. With meat. And a piece of pie."

"And where did Mrs. Crump show you to afterward?"

"A bed with three blankets!"

Jeremy allowed silence to fall between them as Ollie considered his circumstances.

"You would give all that up because of a bath?" Lydia could not help herself. The child looked so determined... but also a little bit lost. "I can't have you visit me for tea if you don't bathe. All proper gentlemen know it's important to smell properly clean when they visit a lady."

At this, she thought she saw Jeremy roll his eyes heavenward.

"But I ain't no proper gentleman," Ollie said.

"Not yet, but with help from Lord Tempest, perhaps

someday you will be one. You could learn to speak and read and write…"

Jeremy appeared as skeptical as Ollie.

But then Ollie loosened his hold on her legs, looking rather torn.

"Go outside and wait for me in the carriage." Jeremy met Ollie's gaze meaningfully. "If you aren't inside of it when I come out, I'll know you've made your choice. You won't be given the same opportunity again."

Ollie fidgeted with a button on the new jacket he was wearing.

"Choose wisely, Ollie," Lydia said.

He glanced up at her, melting her heart with those violet eyes. "You mean it? You really think I could be a gentleman?"

"I do indeed. But you must learn to follow rules first. You must take your baths and do as Mrs. Crump tells you. You are worthy, Ollie, but you cannot run away simply because you're a little uncomfortable. Do you understand?"

Ollie nodded.

"In the carriage, Ollie. At once."

"Yes, sir. I'm sorry, m'lord." He turned to head back toward the kitchen before being halted by Mr. Hill's voice. "Parden me, Mr. Ollie. The carriage is this way."

Ollie turned around in both terror and awe as Mr. Hill reached out his hand and escorted the diminutive little man out the front door.

Likely, it was the first time Ollie had used a front door to enter any sort of home, let alone one of the grandest mansions in all of Mayfair.

CHAPTER 6

"*R*eally, Lydia? A gentleman?" The sarcasm in Jeremy's voice echoed off the ornate walls of the suddenly empty foyer. "I knew you were naïve, but..."

His gaze trailed down her person, and as he did so, the look in his eyes changed from one of derision to something else. They were alone again, and he was as aware of it as she was.

"It is possible." She forced herself to remember what they were discussing. "As a ward of yours."

She expected him to groan or adamantly deny anything of the sort.

"He's to work for me, Lydia." He glanced over his shoulder to where Ollie had disappeared with Mr. Hill. "And we're not off to a very auspicious start."

"He is learning," she pointed out. "It is a beginning."

"He's a little pest."

"He is a pest that you were worried about." Lydia could do nothing to stop the satisfied smile that stretched her lips.

Jeremy stared at the floor, rubbing his chin thoughtfully. "How old would you guess he is?"

The question surprised her. "Five? Six at the most?"

"He is nine, Lydia." Jeremy pinned his gaze back on her. "At least he thinks he is nine. He says he lost track of time after his mother disappeared but believes he was nearing his seventh birthday at the time."

"But he's so small."

Jeremy's eyes darkened. "He only eats what he finds in rubbish bins or what he can steal."

Lydia and Clarissa had discussed this aspect of an orphan's life before. She ought to have realized Ollie was older than he looked.

As horrifying as the reminder was, though, she also felt a sense of peace.

Because Ollie was going to get proper meals now, and Jeremy did not look nearly as cold and cynical, as he had just a few days before. Of course, he was still not the same as he once was; the tragedies of the past year had scarred him. But...

He was not uncaring.

And he had kissed her earlier today—and he'd done it as though he couldn't help himself. He'd been like a man starved.

Much the way she had felt.

Jeremy took a step closer and reached out and brushed his fingertips along the fabric of her sleeve. "How do you manage to look more beautiful each time I see you?"

It didn't feel as though he was complimenting her, more like he was truly baffled by such a phenomenon.

"Jeremy." All she could do was say his name. And of course, all of her feelings sounded in that single word. In that moment, the broken heart she'd lived with since that dreadful November day made itself known as actual physical pain. "What happened? Why do you hate us? Why do you hate me?"

He exhaled loudly, in such a way that she sensed the weight of the world crashing down on him.

"I don't hate you, Lydia." He blinked and turned to stare up at a rather large painting of one of her ancestors. But he wasn't really looking at the painting.

"Then why?"

"I can't tell you why." His voice hardened. "You don't want to know. It wouldn't be fair for me to tell you, nor would it be fair for... others involved."

"My brothers?"

The muscles of his jaw twitched. "And others."

She couldn't help herself, she moved even closer to him until naught but a few inches separated them.

She stared down and grasped both of his hands in hers.

Jeremy's hands were not soft. They never had been. Ever since he'd inherited his father's title, she knew of several occasions when he'd taken the time to work in the fields with his tenants.

He may have been their landlord. They may have feared him a little, even. But they all respected him.

She grazed her fingertips over the callouses, which now sported ink stains.

Jeremy was not an idle person, nor was he a man who accumulated wealth for the sake of accumulating wealth.

He seemed to be lost in his own frenzy, however. Raging against humanity in his grieving.

He did not resist her hold of his hand but neither did he do anything to encourage her.

For Lydia, of course, this was encouragement enough.

Because this was Jeremy.

"I've missed you." She'd wanted to tell him this since she first saw him in Lord Baxter's office and especially while she'd been walking alone with him through the Wicked Earls' Club.

He didn't answer but turned his head away.

She raised one of her hands to trail the line of his jaw. "If you don't hate me, then why...?"

He moved his chin side to side, and then he turned to stare at her again. How many times had she gazed into the warmth of his mahogany gaze, feeling safe and protected, but most of all, simply knowing that he was her destiny?

In that moment, she felt all of this... and more.

Kiss me, she begged him with her eyes. Heat that had once felt like flickering embers burst into a raging inferno.

She pressed up, onto her toes, and parted her lips.

Seeing confusion and indecision in his eyes, she closed her own and waited. She was not afraid that he would embarrass her. Perhaps she ought to be. But she'd also seen something else in his gaze.

She'd seen the same longing that must be reflected in her own.

On tiptoes, one hand cradling his cheek, the other now resting on his shoulder, she waited.

"Lydia." The warmth of his breath fanned her lips. "Lydia."

The temperature of her blood spiked, and a roaring sound filled her ears as it raced through her veins.

Oh, yes. So much yes.

When his mouth captured hers, he seemed to be seeking permission.

And… forgiveness. He was not demanding, impatient, and passionate as he'd been earlier. This kiss was quiet —searching.

When he traced the seam along her lips with his tongue, he did not press inside until she parted her mouth and welcomed all that he would offer.

"Lydia." A shudder ran through him.

Her arms snaked up his chest and encircled his neck now, as though she'd been drowning for months and finally found something to keep her afloat.

Locked in his embrace, sobs threatened to overflow, and her eyes burned with tears.

"Jeremy." Her throat caught. "Why did you hurt me so?" There must be some explanation.

He stilled then, and released her mouth, ending the kiss.

"What did I do wrong?" Her heartache and confusion could not be contained, the question escaping unchecked. She had to know!

He cradled her face in his hands, conflicting emotions burning in his eyes. "I didn't want to. You did nothing." He stared at her mouth and then into her eyes again. "What am I going to do with you, Lydia?"

Love me! Love me! Love me!

These words, however, she kept to herself. He wasn't ready. If she pushed too hard, she'd lose him forever.

But there had to be a way. Deep down, she knew with every fiber of her being that Jeremy loved her as much as she loved him. Anyone else would consider her naïve to convince herself of this, but she didn't care.

She simply knew this about him. *I know him.*

He reached up and, wrapping his fingers around her wrists, extracted himself from their embrace. Stepping back, he closed his eyes as though summoning strength.

Strength to resist her? Or his own urges? His own desires... and dreams?

"Work will begin in the warehouse tomorrow," he said. "I'll have contracts sent over for you to sign in the morning."

When she didn't say anything but only nodded, he took another step backward.

"Ollie is waiting for you," she reminded him.

He made a quick bow and pivoted, his shoes echoing in the vast foyer as he strode toward the door.

He'd kissed her twice yesterday.

Not once, but twice, for God's sake!

Jeremy leaned forward, urging the stallion he'd chosen to ride that morning faster as he raced along the nearly empty road that made up most of Rotten Row. Perhaps the speed could clear his head.

Zeus ate up the ground all too quickly, sending the cool morning air rushing past his face and in his hair.

When Jeremy drew the spirited animal to a halt, the horse protested, throwing back his head and rising momentarily onto his hind legs.

Precisely how Jeremy felt, if he was to be perfectly honest.

The horse lowered his head and then rose up a second time but failed to unseat his rider. Jeremy had been prepared for it, leaning forward and digging his heels into the horse's sides.

Sounds of another rider approaching had Jeremy grimacing until the familiar voice called out.

"Incredible animal!" Baxter was dressed in full morning attire, top hat in place, and riding a white mare who, although nearly as large and haughty as Zeus, was much better mannered.

"He needs work, but he certainly shows promise." Jeremy rubbed his hand along Zeus's slick, black neck as Baxter drew up alongside them.

"Necessary, I know, but I'm almost sorry to see the magnificent ones broken."

Jeremy nodded, agreeing with the sentiment. He turned to ride the length of the row again, and Baxter followed.

"I was going to come by your office today," Jeremy admitted. The park was all but empty and perhaps a better place for this conversation than the club would have been.

"My decision to ride this morning was quite opportune then." The earl sent an approving glance across the space between the two of them. "My countess tells me you're amenable to financing the orphanage."

"Yes." Jeremy marveled that something he'd opposed so vehemently only a few days before had suddenly become one of his top priorities.

"Bash, my brother, has a few concerns about Ludwig."

This caught Jeremy's attention. "Devonshire's considering investing then?"

Baxter scowled and then exhaled loud enough that Jeremy heard it over the pounding of the horses' hooves.

"He and Gold aren't enthusiastic. Aside from some of the shipments known to have gone missing, there are reports that those that have actually arrived at the Ashanti Coast were tampered with. Air pockets are getting caught in the firing chamber. Particularly troublesome when pistols explode in our own soldiers' hands."

Jeremy knew this. And since potential investors did as well...

"Which has effectively driven down Ludwig's value," Jeremy pointed out. "My first objective is to eliminate the vermin involved."

Baxter jerked to a halt and pinned his gaze on Jeremy. "You know who to go after?"

"I have a few leads, and ironically enough, one of them was provided by one of our orphans. A gang boss by the name of Farley. Surely it's not a coincidence that the name Farley has come up on more than one of my manifests?"

"I don't believe in coincidences."

"Not under these circumstances." Jeremy rolled a shoulder. "The Ludwig brothers themselves. are apathetic at best, if not outright culpable. As far as I can tell, they've only encouraged such activity. Impossible for other legitimate businesses to function in the climate that's come about." Legitimate being the keyword.

"There are rumors that they've badgered a few club members. Not good for business at all."

"One way or another, we need to neutralize them."

"My brother mentioned the same." Baxter seemed quite in agreement. "And now with the ladies involved…"

Jeremy nodded. His thoughts exactly. "I'll be thorough. Tell that to your brother and Gold."

"Until then, we can only hope to keep them at bay. But I've no doubt they'll make mischief, if not worse, at the warehouse. They'll fight it. If the children have other options, better options, the gangs lose their soldiers." Baxter stared straight ahead at the unoccupied run.

"One would wonder," Jeremy side-eyed the club owner, "if perhaps you were aware of the connection when you so innocently *suggested* I step in to fund their operations?"

Baxter chortled and then urged his horse forward again. "They don't call me the Earl of Bastards for nothing."

Jeremy could only chuckle at this. And then he wondered if, a few days before, he would have chuckled at anything.

Lydia had always been able to make him laugh when he was feeling dour, and apparently, that hadn't changed.

But it didn't matter. He couldn't allow her to melt his resolve.

She was Lydia, but she was also a Cockfield. And he couldn't look beyond the choice her brothers had made.

"What's really motivating you in all of this, Tempest?" Baxter asked out of the blue, almost as though he was reading Jeremy's mind. "I understand the potential for profits, but in the past two months, you've moved your office to the docks, set your sights on what ought to be a relatively troublesome investment, and now you're intent on rooting out a gang of treasonous villains. It's all well and good, of course, but why now? And why you? Does this have something to do with your brother?"

Jeremy stiffened, and Zeus twitched and then jerked his head, turning sideways on the road and threatening to buck again.

Rather than answer Baxter's question, Jeremy soothed the animal, increasing the pressure with his legs and thighs.

Only when Zeus was under control did he glance at Baxter again.

The earl merely stared at him questioningly, waiting patiently, brows raised.

"My brother served valiantly," Jeremy answered. "Why wouldn't I concern myself with issues that threaten our soldiers?"

Baxter looked as though he knew more but simply tightened his mouth.

"Ludwig's profits will double. Possibly triple," Jeremy continued. He had analyzed every possible scenario and none of the numbers lined up with those provided by the current owners. "The greater the risk, the greater the reward. You, Bash, and Gold are simply going to have to decide if you've the ballocks to go all in."

"It's not me who requires convincing. As I said before..."

"Yes." Jeremy stared knowingly back at the other earl. "However, considering you're known as London's most charmed negotiator, I shouldn't be concerned, eh?"

Baxter snorted. "True."

"And as far as these gang bosses," Jeremy went on, "I've discussed the issue with a handful of Bow Street Runners. But I wouldn't mind a little help with manpower once we decide to raid, once I know more of the specifics."

"How many?"

"Twenty men. More if you can."

"Shouldn't be a problem. Just do me a favor and try to give me a few hours' notice. I'll need to bring substitutes into the club."

Jeremy nodded. The idea that he might be able to clear his brother's name was one he couldn't let go of. Or perhaps, the notion refused to let go of him.

Unfortunately, it was also possible the information he discovered could do just the opposite.

That thought summoned an elephant to sit on his chest.

Damn Lucas, and damn Blackheart, and damn them both to hell that they would turn their backs on his brother so easily.

"Is this orphan of yours the same one you've taken into your home?"

"Women talk too much." But Jeremy nodded.

"Your newfound compassion knows no bounds now."

"Lady Lydia didn't allow me much choice. If I didn't

take him in, she would have taken him home with her to Heart Place. He'd have robbed her blind." Jeremy shrugged. "It's a small thing, and I might as well take advantage of any information he provides me. It won't be long before the boy tires of eanring honest wages. He may lead me right to this Farley fellow."

Lydia would be hugely disappointed, and Jeremy felt an inkling of guilt for not making all of his intentions clear to her. But if he had, she would have only had questions. And she would have defended Ollie most ardently. They would argue. Her cheeks would flush, and her cobalt eyes would sparkle with passion, causing him to forget what they were arguing about in the first place and give into other, counterintuitive urges.

Urges that could only end in further heartache. Jeremy unclenched and clenched his fists. Because both his cock and his heart protested the assumption.

Baxter drew his horse to a halt again and glanced down at his fob watch. "Keep me appraised, Tempest. But I'd best turn back. My countess will be expecting me to break my fast with her." Tipping his hat, he grinned. "Give my best to Lady Lydia."

Jeremy stared after him—a man who, born on the wrong side of the blanket, had elevated himself to become a bloody earl. As the white mare pranced toward the park exit, Baxter road away, his posture as noble as any man born into a title. Damned fellow knew far too much for his own good.

Jeremy couldn't help but wonder what else he knew.

CHAPTER 7

*H*aving met with two seamstresses at Madam Chantal's and arranged for them to make some drawings of potential uniforms, Lydia stood waiting for her driver outside of the Bond Street shop with her maid and exhaled a long sigh.

As busy as she'd kept herself over the past week, it was impossible to keep her mind from going back to the day Jeremy had kissed her.

Twice, he'd kissed her.

Twice.

But since then, it had become quite apparent that he'd decided to avoid her.

Rather than bring the contract to her himself, Jeremy had sent it via messenger. As promised, he had indeed included the requirement that she not visit the Tuesday Warehouse unprotected, and it was an enforceable clause.

But most importantly, the contract ensured that the orphanage would be funded for eighteen months from the date of opening. She could not convince herself the clause was worth arguing over in the face of his generosity.

Even if Jeremy had told her he was only doing this at Baxter's insistence.

Eager to move matters forward, after going over it with her brother's solicitors, Lydia had signed the contract and sent it back the very next day—via messenger as well.

In addition to the contract, Jeremy sent over an ambitious timeline, as well as his preferred contractors. She'd written back that she would like to discuss a few items, but again, two days had since passed without a response.

And he had not once referenced how Ollie was doing in any of them.

Was he avoiding her or his feelings? Or were they one and the same?

She'd seen regret in his eyes after he'd kissed her, and he'd looked almost fearful as he'd backed hastily toward the front door.

Coachman John effectively brought her thoughts to a halt as he pulled the carriage up beside them.

But while she'd been waiting, a pesky little idea had formed in the back of her mind. Would it be so very inappropriate to make an unplanned visit to Jeremy's Townhouse on Cork Street?

To visit Ollie, of course.

She bit her lip.

Visiting an orphan boy she'd taken an interest in ought not to be misconstrued in any way. In fact, it ought to be considered perfectly acceptable. Quite appropriate.

And in the event that she did happen to run into Jeremy, she had her maid with her to act as chaperone.

Nothing improper at all.

Unwilling to rethink her decision, she whipped open the sliding door to the driver's box. "Sixteen Cork Street."

Louise, of course, didn't question their new destination but did raise her brows half an inch.

The truth of the matter was that Lydia was very curious about Ollie's plight. So much so that she'd talked her nerves into settling down considerably by the time they arrived at Jeremy's modest Mayfair townhouse.

Modest by Heart Place standards, that was.

"No need to wait on us, John. Louise and I can return on foot." Knowing her maid was always amenable to taking the air, Lydia waved the carriage away as Louise held the iron gate open for Lydia to pass through.

The brick façade of Jeremy's townhouse was newly painted, and the wood door was polished to a high shine. Oh, she hoped Ollie had made the right decision and stayed with Jeremy after all.

She didn't recognize the servant who opened the door, nor did he recognize her. She faltered, doubting her decision to visit for an instant. Matters between her and Jeremy were very different than they'd been before. She had practically been on a first-name basis with most of his servants at Galewick Manor.

The manservant stared down at her, awaiting some explanation for her visit.

Which in actuality, posed no problem for Lydia. She straightened her spine and lifted her chin. She was a Cockfield, after all.

"I am Lady Lydia Cockfield, sister of the Duke of Blackheart." She summoned some of her brother's demeanor. "I am here to meet with Ollie, the young boy Lord Tempest took in recently."

The butler stared down his nose at her, but then stepped back, widening the door and bowing. "Of course, My Lady. This way, please."

Lydia craned her neck around, taking in her surroundings. This was where Jeremy spent most of his time.

The foyer's decor was very representational of him: subdued but decorated with tasteful paintings, quiet-colored moldings, and shining wood floors. There were several rugs, with simple but elegant floral accents, placed about.

The scent of lemon oil hung in the air as she followed the butler into a drawing room where the walls were painted an eggshell blue and the furnishings upholstered in matching blues and golds. A very expensive-looking vase was propped on a table behind the long settee.

This room, she decided, would have been decorated by his mother.

"How is Lady Tempest," she asked impulsively.

The butler frowned as though uncertain of divulging his employer's personal information.

"My dear Aunt Emma asked me to inquire." Involving one's dear aunt into any occasion was certain to lend an air of respectability.

And apparently it did.

"She is improving. Her doctors are cautiously optimistic." And then the butler clutched his hands behind his back. "Do make yourself comfortable, My Lady. I'll have the boy brought down immediately, and if it is to your liking, your maid may wait in the kitchens with Mrs. Crump. Do not hesitate to use the bell pull if you have need of anything. I am Mr. Bartholomew, at your service."

Louise glanced questioningly over at Lydia.

"I am not in need of a chaperone while visiting with a nine-year-old boy." She smiled, knowing her maid would likely take tea with the servants below, and that she would enjoy that far more than sitting in a corner watching her fuss over Ollie.

As Louise all but flew out of the room, Lydia turned back to Mr. Bartholomew. "You said he would be 'brought down'?" She'd have thought he'd be working below stairs.

"From the nursery, my lady."

"Oh… thank you, Mr. Bartholomew." Surely, Ollie would not be spending time in the nursery if he was also a servant? Pleasant tingles swirled in her chest as she contemplated the various possibilities of what this meant.

She could not sit down. She could not relax.

This was Jeremy's home. A home she might once have become mistress of but for some unknown reason that was being kept secret from her.

If she was to suffer because of it, for goodness sakes, she deserved to know the details.

If Lucinda was here, she'd surely find out. Lucinda would make everyone miserable until she had every last detail.

A sudden wave of longing crashed over her; there were times when her twin sister's absence felt like a missing limb—or, at least, how she imagined one would be. She wondered if Lucinda was feeling the same way or if she was too distracted with her new husband...

With some effort, she forcibly shifted her thoughts away from the lingering melancholy and back to the matter at hand. She was here now to check on Ollie and possibly Jeremy, if he was at home, that is, and if he would let her.

Lydia paced across the floor and then stopped to stare out a window facing the gardens. It was three in the afternoon. Was Jeremy meeting with one of his employees at the warehouse without her? Or was he at his office, going over numbers and contemplating new ventures to keep himself distracted from annoying ladies he'd once nearly been engaged to?

Lydia wouldn't put it past him to be tucked away in his study, hiding from her.

Because surely, if he was here, his butler would inform him that he had a guest.

She sighed just as the door opened and Ollie appeared. Wearing short pants and a white shirt with a laced collar, he was accompanied by a tall, slim woman who looked to be in her late forties. Lydia had seen enough women in this profession to know his companion was a governess. She had that air of authority combined with a no-nonsense presence. Ollie moved to lurch forward but was caught firmly by the woman's hand on his shoulder.

"Make your bow to Her Ladyship, Master Oliver."

The woman's voice commanded, but Lydia was pleased to also hear a note of affection.

Jeremy had hired a governess for Ollie!

All the warmth of summer swept through her.

Ollie bowed low, folding over completely to where he nearly lost his balance, and then rose. He glanced backward then as though asking his governess if he'd performed the gesture appropriately.

"Very good, Master Oliver." The governess nodded in approval.

Lydia rose. "Thank you, Miss…?"

"Mrs. Mumford."

"You are Ollie's… governess?"

"I am, my lady."

This was most unexpected!

As much as she wanted to pick the woman's mind as to how she'd come by her position and what her instructions were regarding Ollie, her purpose for coming was to ask Ollie how he was doing. He might not be straightforward with her when another adult was present.

"I thank you for bringing him down, Mrs. Mumford. I'll send him back upstairs to resume your daily schedule as soon as Oliver and I are done chatting."

"Very well, my lady. We have not yet completed our handwriting exercises today." She stepped backward. "I will take my tea and return to collect him."

Lydia smiled down at Ollie as the governess took her leave. So many changes might be exciting for him but might also be overwhelming.

Lowering herself onto a settee, she gestured for Ollie

to take the place beside her. "Won't you sit down with me?."

He squirmed and tugged at his collar but did as she asked, those violet eyes flashing around the room and filled with curiosity.

"All of this is very different from what you are used to, isn't it?"

He turned his gaze back to her. "I didn't expect none of this."

Taking responsibility for an orphan could not be so simple as this. "I'm glad you decided to stay with his Lordship. I would have worried if you'd done otherwise."

Ollie bounced restlessly, his hands flat beside him on the cushions. "When's he sendin' me back, do ya ken? I have to make sure me brother ain't gettin' into too much barney."

"Barney? I don't know what you mean." Nor had she realized he had a brother. "Does Lord Tempest know about your brother?"

"He does, m'lady. Says he'll find him too. But I don't think he can. If Buck don't wanna be found, ain't no one who can. Except for Farley. He can find anyone. He knows all the bloomin' hidin' places."

"Does Buck need to hide a lot?" Ollie had mentioned this Buck boy before.

Ollie plucked a small figurine of two small boys off the table and rubbed his fingertips along the smooth carving. "Yeah, he does. He's older than me."

Ollie was worried about his brother. A brother, who, apparently, got into a good deal of barney.

"How old is Buck?"

"He's four and ten."

Five years older than Ollie; he must be considerably larger. And she remembered Ollie telling them that Buck had been the one to cause the bruises when they'd discovered him in the warehouse. "I'm sure Buck is fine, then. And if Lord Tempest says he's going to find him, I've no doubt that he will."

Ollie tilted his head sideways. "Buck's always messin' up. And fightin' when I'm not there to talk him outta it. Got his face right cut up past winter."

"You are not responsible for what your brother does," Lydia said, patting his leg.

Ollie sighed, eyebrows crinkled in an expression that looked too old for his small face. "He's my brother, I can't help it."

The floor creaked, and Lydia glanced up. She had not heard Jeremy enter the room. For a moment, his eyes looked almost haunted, but the expression flickered and disappeared when he dipped his chin in her direction.

Lydia licked her lips, staring at his bared arms where his shirt sleeves were rolled up. He must have been working in his study after all.

Every button on his silk gold waistcoat was fastened, and the bottoms of his buff breeches were neatly tucked into shining Hessians.

"Mr. Bartholomew informed me that you…" Jeremy gestured behind him, almost as though providing a reason for his appearance. "I did not realize we had a meeting."

"We did not," Lydia answered.

Jeremy cocked a brow.

"I came to have a visit with *Master Oliver*," Lydia explained.

Nothing in the world could hold back her pleasure at Ollie's elevated circumstances. But she could not tease Jeremy about this or gloat. What on earth had transpired to cause Jeremy to decide to raise Ollie as a ward and not a servant?

"Mrs. Mumford is waiting in the foyer for you, Oliver." Jeremy's voice was cool and commanding.

Ollie hopped up, but when he moved toward the door, Jeremy stopped him with a question. "Did your letters give you as much difficulty this morning?"

Ollie shook his head. "Not so hard as the day before. Yer tricks ya told me helped."

"Very good." Jeremy's lips twitched, and Ollie's mouth stretched into a wide grin before he scrambled across the room. After struggling only slightly to pull the heavy door open, he exited and then very purposefully pushed it closed behind him, leaving Lydia alone with Jeremy for the first time in nearly a week.

Jeremy had not moved from where he stood, feet planted wide, hands behind his back.

He looked very much the Earl of Tempest today. Imposing, haughty...

Adorably austere.

"Please, don't tell me you came here without a companion," he said.

"My maid is in the kitchen with your housekeeper, taking tea." And since he appeared to be quite at a loss, Lydia folded her hands in her lap graciously. "Won't you sit down?" she invited for the second time in less than a quarter of an hour.

…while sitting in a drawing room that was not her own.

She wasn't going to allow him to chase her away so easily this time. She never ought to have allowed him to chase her away to begin with.

To her surprise, Jeremy took the place Ollie had vacated. If he'd wanted to continue avoiding her, he easily could have claimed the winged-back chair on the opposite side of the room.

"Ollie says he has a brother. Have you had any luck finding him?"

"Buck. And yes, I have." Jeremy stared down at his hands and her gaze followed.

Slim and masculine with a few curling tendrils of black hair on his knuckles, she couldn't help but notice how sinewy muscle flexed and moved beneath his skin. Lydia clutched her hands tightly in her lap, squashing the desire to trail her fingers along his forearm… all the way to where it disappeared beneath the folds of his sleeves.

"Lydia?" He was watching her now.

She sat up straight and pressed her knees together. "I'm sorry. You were saying?"

But he was watching her knowingly. Of course, she could never hide her feelings from anyone.

"You found Buck?" she persisted.

"Ah, yes." Jeremy frowned. "He's… trouble. Far more trouble than Ollie ever would have been. If Ollie's going to stand half a chance at a proper life, the older boy can't remain a part of his life."

"Oh…" She hated that Buck had beaten on Ollie, but they couldn't very well keep Ollie from his brother indefinitely, could they? "But he's Ollie's brother."

Pain showed in Jeremy's eyes, and Lydia guessed that memories of his own brother had come to mind.

"I miss Lucinda every day," she confessed. "But I know she is happy and well. I can't imagine what it's like to be denied a sibling."

She'd stood beside him at his brother's funeral and watched him grieve. But he had survived. He'd not hated her brothers then—two men who might provide some of the companionship he missed now.

Jeremy's throat pulsed. "Buck will ruin Ollie if he remains in his life."

Of course, he must be right. "What will you tell Ollie?"

"The truth—that he has a choice."

It was a very, very hard choice to present to one so young. In fact, it was a nigh impossible one.

"So, he's going to have to choose between his own well-being—his own chance at living a meaningful and productive life—and staying at his brother's side. I'm not sure he'll be able to do that. I know that I couldn't."

"That's why I…" Jeremy shook his head dismissively. "I'll send for your maid." He moved to rise but Lydia stopped him, placing her hand on his thigh.

"That's why you what?" she asked, sensing he'd nearly told her something very important. "That's why you what, Jeremy?"

CHAPTER 8

*J*eremy winced.

He'd damn near spilled his bleeding heart.

"Please, Jeremy. I need to know." Lydia's hands gripped above his knees. Seeing the lace of her gloves, her delicate hands resting on his thighs, had him... floundering.

A sensation that in anyone else's presence was a foreign one.

If she moved her hands just a few inches higher... He closed his eyes. "I don't want you to have to decide. It would not have been fair."

"Decide what, between my brothers and... myself?" She squeezed hard, her fingers digging into his muscles. "*Tell me*, Jeremy. Tell me so that I can understand. Tell me so I can either fix whatever it is that's caused you to hate all of us or move forward without you."

"You can't fix it. No one can fix it. Don't you think that if anyone could, I would have done that already?"

But perhaps he could tell her some of it. He could tell her just enough so that she could forget about him—forget about the past.

He drew in a sharp breath. He'd let go of her four months ago, and it had hurt like hell. Watching her find someone else... The sharp breath evolved into a painful ache.

"I never wanted you to have to choose between your family and me." He kept his eyes lowered, unable to look at her. But that was all he would say. It was all he *could say.*

Because the reason had to do with so much more than just himself. It had to do with the honor of his family, the betrayal of her brothers, and most importantly, his brother's memory.

He'd been livid after hearing Lucas' suspicions. Arthur would never commit treason. *His brother had not been a traitor.*

Shame and guilt attacked him for even considering it. *Damn* Lucas. *Damn* Blackheart.

Damnit, Arthur!

"But why...?" The bewildered pain in her voice had him staring into her eyes, glistening with confused tears, making them look more emerald than blue.

She was completely separate from all of those reasons and yet they had changed the course of her life.

"It has nothing to do with you." His voice caught.

"But, Jeremy. You are wrong." One of those tears overflowed and trailed down to the corner of her mouth. *"It has everything to do with me—with us."*

He sat frozen, loyalty to his brother warring with his

heart. Because she was right. Their future together had been shattered by Lucas and Blackheart's betrayal. By her brothers' deplorable accusations.

Arthur was his flesh and blood. *His brother would never...*

Shifting his gaze to the window, the desire to kiss away her tears nearly broke him.

"Please, Jeremy?"

"Your brothers..." It was all he could say. "I can't—"

"But it is my brothers you are angry with. It isn't me that you hate."

"God, Lydia, I could never hate you." Quite the opposite.

Was he telling her too much? Was he making this worse than it already was?

"You told me to stay away from you." A hint of accusation flashed in her gaze. Deserved. Well deserved.

"You need to... allow me to complete the renovations for the orphanage. Allow me to do this for you while you attend balls, garden parties, and river parties. We... Us. Cannot happen. An arrangement between the two of us is impossible."

He'd said it. So, why didn't he experience any relief?

"Impossible?"

One of her hands slid up to his groin, and he practically burst into flames. She wasn't touching him, but she was close.

"Lydia." He grasped her wrist.

"I am unconvinced."

She was more stubborn than she had been last spring. In that short time since he'd sent her away, she had changed from a demure young lady to a headstrong woman.

And God in heaven, she was even more tempting now. More beautiful. More powerful.

Utterly irresistible.

Her fingers uncurled beneath his hand and splayed over the fabric of his trousers, dangerously grazing the stretched material confining his damned unruly cock.

She leaned in. "I'm not a child to be kept locked away, to be protected from the ugliness in the world." Her voice sounded throaty... sensual.

Her pupils were dilated, diminishing the blue so that the glints in her eyes were like stars in a moonless sky. Her softly rounded cheeks were flushed, heated. And her lips...

Her lips were parted, shining, and inviting him to do things he doubted she even knew possible. He stared past them, into the darker reds and tender textures, imagining other flesh he craved to know.

"You don't hate me," she insisted, leaning in, her hands resting on his arm, sweet breath fanning his jaw.

"No." He clenched his fists, willing his heart to slow.

And then she touched her tongue to his earlobe.

"Lydia."

"Tell me again this is impossible," she demanded in a whisper. "I dare you to convince me."

His willpower, which he'd always considered iron-clad, chose that moment to shatter most spectacularly. Faster than lightning, Jeremy had her seated across his lap, one arm behind her and the other roving over her arms, the curve of her hip.

"*You* are impossible," he said. "Damnit, it's you."

He'd tried, by god, he'd tried. He claimed her mouth and then deepened their kiss. Her whimper vibrated between them.

"Not impossible," she countered when he released her mouth to trail kisses down her neck.

But the two of them, together, like this, was in fact, impossible.

A voice of reason raged inside his head, even as his heart sang and his body breathed giant gulps of relief to hold her again.

He'd felt dead inside for so long. He would pay later for giving in to these emotions. He should push her away, run out the door as far as his feet would take him.

Except this was his house.

"Lydia," he sighed, his hands wandering over her supple curves. How had he imagined he could live without her?

He'd clung to his need to absolve Arthur's name. But he'd not been living. He'd merely been existing.

Her hands snaked around his neck, and she turned to face him, placing herself in an even more inappropriate position.

Knees bent, bracketing his thighs.

By god, she was straddling him.

This. How long had he needed this?

Needed her?

Memories of when she was a young girl flitted through his mind—and earlier that year, when she'd stood beside him at his brother's funeral, when she'd met him on the bridge that separated his property from her brother's, when she'd hesitantly given him permission to kiss her.

He'd known Lydia for most of his life. And all the while, he'd expected to marry her.

Knowing what awaited the two of them had been akin to living with a wonderful promise—a promise that his future held good things.

Wonderful things.

Without the promise of that future, all color had drained out of his life.

He stroked her silk-clad ankles, hidden in her skirts. Locating the small indents there, he traced his fingertips over them. So fragile. Feminine.

Sensual.

He then ghosted his palms over her calves, rounded her knees, and edged them up the length of her thighs.

All hidden in the billowing fabric of her skirt. Hidden treasure.

"I need you, Jeremy." She slowly rolled her hips against him.

She could not know what she was saying—what she was doing.

"So badly." She exhaled.

The heat of her center pressed down on the bulge in his trousers. Trouble. She was steering them headlong into trouble. And rather than drop anchor, he raised the sails, intent on traveling full speed ahead.

He'd deal with the trouble when they got there.

Jeremy tugged at her sleeves and lowered her bodice. How many times had he dreamed of doing this while courting her? Soft, creamy skin captured his gaze. A pink flush appeared, and he groaned.

The reality of Lydia in his arms, of her flesh bared beneath his gaze, surpassed any dream he could concoct on his own.

His prim and proper debutante was rocking against him. As he laved and suckled and nipped with his teeth, he realized that he had indeed been correct in the assumption he'd made before.

Because Lydia Cockfield did, in fact, taste like love.

LOST in the haze of this… wanting, Lydia knew she should stop. *Ladies do not do this.*

Not in the privacy of an isolated meadow, not in an earl's Mayfair townhouse, and most definitely not with a gentleman who was not her husband.

But… this was Jeremy.

"Oh," she gasped.

His mouth summoned hot jumpy sensations… all over. She wanted closer to him.

She was well aware of how a woman and a man came together—in the dark, in a bedchamber, the lady in her nightdress, the man wearing… Well, she wasn't certain of that, but she knew that he'd eventually be…

Exposed.

Jeremy's body was hard precisely where she needed him to feel hard. Caught up in the pressure building between the two of them, she imagined all manner of scenarios. Some that involved activities that would resemble the marriage act and others that were, well... unimaginable. Only she did imagine them. Even now...

Frantic, she lowered her hands to his falls but before she could begin to unfasten them, he stopped her.

He was right here. She was in his arms and yet...

He was unreachable.

"Not... like this." His voice came out gravelly, rough.

She lifted her lashes to stare into his eyes, her lids heavy as she struggled to focus.

"But..." Was that her making that whining sound?

His gaze pinned on her, he jerked his hips up and prodded... Precisely where she ached to be prodded.

"Like this."

She could barely hold her head up.

He pulsed upward again, and then again, building on the friction she'd been chasing.

"Jeremy." Her head fell back this time, and she would have fallen off his lap if his hands weren't gripping her waist. He'd located her center and felt harder than before. Like wood, like steel, he ignited more heat—more wanting. White light danced over her skin at the same time little bursts of lightning sped through her veins.

"Let go, sweet, like that."

Let go.

Let go?

Wasn't that what she was doing?

The settee was shaking now, knocking against the table behind it. His butler or housekeeper could come along any moment, wanting to know what on earth was happening in here.

She allowed herself a split second to glance toward

the closed door and when she swung her gaze back to him, she was surprised to see a bead of perspiration dotting his brow.

"What if someone comes?" she asked.

"Precisely what I'm hoping for." His eyes flashed teasingly but then closed again, and squeezing her hips tightly, he growled.

The knocking sounds grew louder as his thrusts carried her closer…

Closer to… something.

And then she doubted she'd care if King George himself strode through the door.

Jeremy shuttered, something shattered, and then the most compelling feeling of completion rolled over her. At some point, she'd fallen forward, and they were all but gasping into one another's mouths.

"Jeremy."

"Are you all right, sweets?"

"I am, but…"

"What is it?" He stared at her in concern.

"The vase. I think we broke the vase."

And in that moment, her hope that everything was going to turn out perfectly fine grew even stronger.

Because Jeremy Gilcrest threw back his head and laughed.

CHAPTER 9

"*L*ord Tempest, Baxter." The younger of the two elderly Ludwig Bros. stepped forward, hand outstretched as Jeremy and Baxter, as well as their men of business, entered the spacious but shabby meeting room housed in the Ludwig Bros. Shipping offices. If everything went as planned, the sale would be finalized by the end of this meeting.

Both Ludwig brothers were well beyond their seventies, and Jeremy knew that neither of them had any family other than one another. Despite the fact that one was considerably plumper than the other, they were nearly identical. Both were balding with white hair, parchment-like complexions, and watery blue eyes.

Seeing the brothers together elicited a painful twisting in Jeremy's heart. It was a reminder that Arthur would never work beside him in business. They wouldn't grow old together. His own brother would forever be a young man in his memory.

Jeremy cleared his throat and pushed the thought

away before lowering himself into the chair beside Baxter.

"I'm Leo, and this old grump of a fellow is Rudolph," Leo quipped before taking his seat at the table. Based on the delivery of the joke, as well as Rudolph's unimpressed grunt, Jeremy had no doubt Leo had been using the same line for most of their adult lives.

At the far end of the table, Rudolph didn't bother glancing up from what he was reading. Addendums to the contract—a rather satisfying collection of them. Jeremy flicked his glance over the thick binder of documents that he himself had compiled and then leaned back and crossed one foot over his knee. Was he anxious to get this over with? Yes. Would he show it? Hell, no.

"We can't all be the charming ones." Baxter threw a quick glance in Jeremy's direction, and Leo laughed.

"Makes you and I look even better, eh, Baxter?" Leo agreed. "I'd offer you a smoke, but perhaps we should wait until after the negotiations?"

"Brilliant, Leo, as usual," Rudolph muttered without looking up from his reading.

A handful of begrudging-looking gentlemen, presumably the Ludwigs' solicitors, leaned against the wall, almost like soldiers but with their arms folded across their chests. They took their turns nodding as Leo Ludwig made introductions, but all the while Jeremy kept his gaze pinned on the grumpy one. Rudolph Ludwig would be the one to bring up all objections and questions.

Baxter took the seat beside Jeremy and then caught his gaze meaningfully. Although the club owner had, in fact, brought in considerable investment money, Jeremy would be the major shareholder, maintaining ownership of fifty-one percent. For that reason, and because he was the most informed, he would act as principal negotiator.

After waiting nearly half a minute, Rudolph finally raised his head and leveled his watery gaze on Jeremy. "This isn't the asking price."

The room fell silent at the gambit, and Jeremy immediately recognized his advantage.

These penny-pinching merchants considered gentlemen of the nobility to be foolish and cavalier where business was concerned. Jeremy was happy to be underestimated.

"It's twenty percent more than the company's worth." Ten percent, but that was beside the point.

Jeremy would rather not bring up the missing ammunition nor the arms that had been tampered with.

But if necessary, he would.

Rudolph grunted, placed an unlit cigar between his teeth, and turned the page. "This ship is undervalued," he said around the cigar.

Jeremy opened his own folder and offered the evaluation he'd had done. "I beg to differ. Unless you have documentation proving otherwise?"

Rudolph only grunted again, and then went on to dispute something else.

Two and a half hours later, having made zero allowances where price was concerned, Jeremy and Baxter stepped onto the docks as the new owners of one of England's oldest shipping companies. Official paperwork in hand, Jeremy stared up at the gray and cloudy sky and waited for relief that didn't come.

Buying Ludwig Bros. was only the first step in clearing Arthur's name. Tomorrow, he'd begin the task of sifting through the company's original accounting records. It would be one of those undertakings where finding nothing would be considered a good thing.

He'd sift out the traitors, bring them to justice, and there would be no mention of his brother.

Would he find relief then? Would it be enough?

Arthur had not been a saint. Arthur had just been... Arthur: the charming brother, the ladies' man. Yes, he had cheated on his wife and then failed to take the necessary steps to provide properly for his daughter, but he wasn't a traitor.

Jeremy was certain of this.

NONE of this would have been necessary if Lucas and Blackheart had simply left well enough alone. Jeremy wouldn't have had to remain in London over the winter, putting his mother's health at risk; he wouldn't have had to buy a damn shipping company nor would he have been forced to go to war with an army of dock thieves.

And he'd already be married to Lydia.

Lydia, without whom, he was coming to realize, his life was nothing more than a series of monotonous days.

And endless, frustrating nights

And having come to that conclusion, he realized he was going to have to change the way he'd been thinking.

His gut roiled at the thought of enduring their betrayal, but Lydia was worth it.

She always had been.

He could never esteem her brothers as he once had. Not after all of this. But for her sake, for both their sakes, he would learn to tolerate them as brothers-in-law.

He simply needed proof to convince Lucas to call off the official investigation he'd set into motion through the War Office.

"I'd suggest we go for a drink, but Clarissa will want me home early," Baxter said, smiling in satisfaction. "She tends to get this way every time we host a dinner party. You are coming, aren't you?"

"I said I would, didn't I?"

There were six other investors and, from what the earl told him, his wife had invited them all: Baxter's brother, Devonshire—or Bash as he called him—the Earl of Goldthwaite, the Earl of Westerley, Baron Chaswick, and the Marquess of Greystone. It wouldn't look good for Jeremy to forgo the event, as much as he'd like to.

"It seems you're finally learning, Tempest," Baxter observed as Jeremy's carriage appeared.

Blasted Baxter—his notions regarding amiability were wearing Jeremy down.

And yet, his mouth tipped up in a sly smile. Because Lydia, who he had not seen for three days, was going to be in attendance.

After denying himself her company for four months with every intention of doing so indefinitely, he could now barely go three days without her.

Without tasting her. Or kissing her. Or participating

in other undignified, unmentionable, satisfying, yet unsatisfying exploits with her.

She'd been dismayed over the broken vase. Beyond dismayed when she'd learned that it had been produced in China sometime during the Tang Dynasty. Jeremy had refused to confirm that it had been almost a thousand years old, but she'd nearly collapsed with the vapors anyway.

His mother, on the other hand, might have something else to say about it once she was recovered. He would have to purchase a replica.

Caring for something so mundane gave him pause. Was Lydia dragging him out of the clawing darkness he'd muddled through all year?

Suddenly, everything in his life seemed to revolve around her. And if felt right.

It felt righter than anything had in a very long time.

Seated in the forward-facing bench, Baxter stared out the window, his arms crossed and his legs sprawled between them.

Jeremy would relay the earl to his Mayfair home first, so the man could settle his wife's nerves before her dinner party and then he would have his driver return him to Bond Street. The decision to visit Rundell and Bridge's—the jewelers—was an impulsive one.

He would be prepared when all of this worked out. *If* all of this worked out.

If the original records had not been destroyed.

If his brother's name wasn't listed amongst the other blackguards.

And if the proof was enough to convince Lucas and Blackheart to stand down.

Jeremy inhaled a shaky breath. That was a long list of ifs.

For the first time in over a year, he was beginning to believe his future held something other than grief and hopelessness.

Because when Lydia had stepped into his life again, she'd brought hope along with her.

Hope.

It was a terrifying thing.

LYDIA TRAILED her gaze around the elegant but crowded drawing room. Clarissa's dinner party was not the intimate gathering Lydia had assumed it would be. With all of Jeremy's investors present, as well as their respective wives, the evening promised to be more of a grand celebration. Apparently, the purchase of Ludwig Bros. Shipping had gone better than planned,

"This Season promises to be considerably quieter than last spring, what with the Ravensdale brothers married off, as well as... a few other handsome rogues." Lady Greystone's gaze drifted across the room, and she smiled over her glass. Lydia decided that the well dressed and very handsome man she stared at must be her husband, the Marquess of Greystone.

If Lydia realized nothing else that evening, the couples among Clarissa's guests ought to be sufficient to convince her that happy endings were indeed possible.

Every single lady here appeared beyond content, and their Lordly husbands seemed quite taken with their wives.

One of them, Lady Westerley, a pretty American with startling red hair who was obviously with child, hardly went more than ten minutes without her husband crossing the room to inquire as to her health. That he was willing to break from society's norms was not only sweet but touching.

Because it was one thing for Lady Westerley to appear in public in her condition but quite another for her husband, who was also an earl, to be living in her pocket.

And yet... Lydia felt quite comfortable amongst them.

All of the ladies were kind and welcoming. And although every gentleman present was titled in one way or another, Lydia quickly gathered that this event was not really a *tonish* one at all.

It was more of a business affair—business among friends—if she were to go by the bits of conversation she'd taken part in so far.

Lydia swallowed a sip of the sherry Lord Baxter had procured for her and glanced toward the door for the hundredth time. *Where is he?*

Clarissa intercepted her gaze and winced.

When the countess had visited, two days before, and Lydia told her she'd seen Jeremy again, Clarissa had guessed as to most of the details of their meeting. Most of the general details, anyhow. Lydia had not relayed that she had sat on Jeremy's lap, nor what she'd done while she'd sat there.

Clarissa had dissolved into a fit of giggles when she told her about the vase.

Lydia had burst off of Jeremy and tried collecting the pieces, hoping there was some way the vase could be patched together, but repairing it had been impossible, and Jeremy had knelt beside her on the floor and halted her efforts.

"What's done is done," he'd said. "No use hurting yourself trying to glue it back together." And then he'd drawn her back to sit beside him on the comfortable settee and settled his arm around her shoulders.

Lydia had been certain his butler would interrupt them, especially after hearing the sound of shattering porcelain. But they had been left alone.

Leaving her to contemplate what the two of them had done and what it had meant.

To cover for her nervousness, she'd asked him about Ollie and then described the uniforms to be sewn. He'd grown suspiciously silent, so with nothing else to babble about, she'd leapt up from the settee and made to leave.

And of course, he'd insisted on driving her home. "I don't know what Blackheart was thinking leaving you for so long without protection," he pointed out yet again.

Lydia had not reminded him that if her brother was here, there was no way she'd have been left alone with him that afternoon.

And if they had not been left alone, they would not have done... whatever that was called. It had not been intercourse and most assuredly went far beyond kissing. It had simply been...

Wicked.

"What are you thinking?" he'd asked while they'd waited in the foyer for his carriage to be brought around. She had answered with nothing more than a mysterious smile. When he had not raised the subject of the nature of their relationship, she'd not broached it either.

Three days had passed since that afternoon in his drawing room on Cork Street, and she'd not seen or heard from him even once.

"Is he the Earl of Tempest?" Lady Westerley asked, flicking her gaze toward the door discreetly.

The sound of Jeremy's name summoned Lydia's attention immediately.

She twisted around again, and at last, the evening held promise.

"Yes," Lydia answered. "That's him."

CHAPTER 10

*L*ydia watched as his gaze scanned the room and the moment it landed on her, he paused, and his eyes warmed to the color of dark chocolate.

He'd told her that the two of them, together, were impossible, but he was wrong. The hint of a smile dancing on his lips sent tingles racing down her spine. Not impossible at all.

When Lord Westerley stepped forward to greet Jeremy, congratulating hand outstretched, the almost unworldly connection between her and Jeremy was broken, leaving Lydia feeling momentarily bereft.

And then she realized that this was something of a special moment for him.

Her disappointment was swept away and replaced with unexpected pleasure.

The other gentlemen guests stepped forward as well to express their appreciation, and he was quickly surrounded. Slaps on the back ensued, and Westerley pressed a glass into his hand.

When Lydia next managed to catch a glimpse of the man of the hour, she almost laughed out loud at his expression of confusion and disbelief. He hadn't expected this. Lydia held herself back, happy to witness his triumph.

She didn't really understand the significance of purchasing a shipping company, or why it had been so important, but it was obvious he'd met with great success. Watching him absorb the honor of his contemporaries warmed her heart.

Lady Westerley had edged up beside her and Lydia couldn't help but ask, "I realize they are all invested, but they have not profited yet, have they?"

"It's because Lord Tempest intends to not only stop the smugglers who've been operating through Ludwig Bros., but he also intends to bring them to justice. In the past few years, the gang bosses have widened their territory beyond the docks—to the clubs and to legal trade. Westerley says that they'll never contain these types of criminals completely, but Lord Tempest... Well, he's tackled the root of it. I rather believe that this—" she waved her hand toward the doorway where the men were gathered "—isn't only about the investment but signifies their support."

Lydia watched the group of men who appeared ridiculously confident, if not outright cocky, and exhaled a sigh of relief.

He did not have to do everything alone—even if he'd ended his friendship with her brothers. She was happy for him, but she was also a little sad.

What had Lucas and Blackheart done to him? And

then another question niggled in her mind. Was it possible that Jeremy's involvement in the docks was connected to Lucas and Blackheart? She had heard them discussing Ludwig Bros. Shipping and wished now that she'd bothered to actually pay attention.

Jeremy's brother, Arthur, had been killed thousands of miles away, but the insurgents had ambushed them to take away their weapons. Weapons that might have been shipped to them by Ludwig Brothers, perhaps?

"Do the gang bosses smuggle weapons?" Lydia asked.

"Mostly," Lady Westerley answered. "That and various libations."

Lord and Lady Baxter's manservant chose that moment to announce dinner, and all of her rational thoughts fled when, freed up at last, Jeremy strolled in her direction from across the room. Lady Westerley offered him her own congratulations and then joined her husband, leaving Lydia and Jeremy alone.

He was quiet as the two of them stood watching the other couples drift out of the drawing room, and Lydia did not feel the need to press, sensing he required a moment to ground himself.

Not until everyone else had exited did Jeremy tuck her arm into his and lead her toward the door.

With two actual dukes in attendance, a room full of countesses, and a baroness, Lydia felt positively outranked for one of the first times in her life.

"You look stunning tonight." Lydia jumped when his breath caressed the side of her face. "You were born to wear that color of blue".

She'd chosen the gown intentionally. "I remember it's

your favorite." She glanced down, feeling warmth flood her cheeks.

"Cobalt. The first time I stared into your eyes, I thought my own were tricking me."

"No tricks." She felt like humming beside him. She had missed this! And yet another layer had been added to their relationship; something electric now vibrated beneath their conversation.

She'd not really... flirted with him before. They'd been friends who held deep affection for one another. But also, there had been a certainty to their match. Or so she'd believed.

"You cannot have been more than six." He chuckled. "And, God, but that makes me feel old."

"You are not old." She squeezed his arm. "You were eighteen at the time and just returned from school to visit Blackheart." Her parents had been gone for two years already. "You took tea with Lucinda and me. But you refused to hold my doll."

"Your brothers never would have let me hear the end of it. As it was..." He bit off what he'd been going to say, almost as though he'd forgotten he despised them now. But surely, he could not despise them forever, could he?

They entered the long dining room, and he dropped her hand in order to draw out a chair for her to sit in. A single seat that was flanked by chairs occupied by the Duchess of Goldthwaite and Baron Chaswick.

He made a quick bow and then left her to take a seat at the opposite end of the room.

The mention of Blackheart must have reminded him that he had intended to keep away from her.

She lessened her disappointment by telling herself that at least now, he seemed to be torn, and that was far better than his frame of mind four months ago.

And if the heated glances he persistently sent in her direction were anything to go by, it was possible that his feelings for her had a chance at winning the battle in the end.

She hoped, anyhow.

∼

"WOULD you mind driving Lady Lydia home this evening? Her driver's horse... er... threw a shoe and had to return to Heart Place early?"

"It threw a shoe in your drive?"

The Countess of Baxter shrugged. "I've been telling Baxter that we needed to repair it."

"Of course." He chuckled. "I am at your service."

He'd successfully evaded Lydia for most of the evening. Jeremy had been the one to bring up Blackheart, and he'd caught himself all but reminiscing, speaking of the man fondly.

With his objectives unbalanced, he'd avoided her, which hadn't been fair of him. She deserved better—she always had.

And fool that he was, in the end, he'd suffered for it and wasn't at all certain that he'd actually been successful. Because he couldn't keep from appreciating her even at a distance. Her hair shone like ebony silk, the flush of her cheeks reminded him of pink and white roses, and not only did her gown match the color of her eyes, but it hinted at the lush curves he'd found himself craving late at night.

And craving in the morning.

And craving at other most inopportune moments.

He wasn't the sort of man to vacillate with his intentions. He never had been.

In truth, guessing that Lady Baxter had sent Lydia's coach home herself, doing a bit of matchmaking, Jeremy conceded that he ought to be thanking the clever countess.

No more indecisiveness.

He wanted her in his life regardless of what her brothers had done. He would live with the consequences —for her.

He would come to terms with the knowledge that by giving into his heart, he would sacrifice a piece of his family's honor.

He'd do the one thing he'd sworn he never would: betray his brother.

But Lydia would be in his life again. And he needed her.

He exhaled, shakily.

"Clarissa says my driver had to leave early and that you've offered to provide me with a ride?" The object of his thoughts appeared in the foyer, looking tentative and a little confused. "Mr. Smith is fetching my coat and then I'll be ready to leave."

"Very good." Her scent rose up to tantalize him, the sweetest of flowers. The drive would be a short one, but they would be alone.

"Are you in danger?" Her question had Jeremy

glancing at her curiously.

"Why would you think that?"

"Because you've taken on these dock criminals. They cannot be happy about your interference." Her brows lowered in concern. "I knew dealing with them would become necessary eventually, but I had thought it was mostly children... Like Ollie's brother, and their friends."

He didn't want to lie to her, but neither did he want for her to worry.

Baxter's butler approached, however, successfully preventing Jeremy from having to do either.

"Your carriage awaits in front, My Lord." The butler turned. "Your coat, My Lady."

Jeremy intercepted Lydia's coat and held it up. When her gaze met his, he felt more than a little sheepish, remembering that he'd intentionally refrained from helping her into her coat not too long ago at the Wicked Earls' Club. Instinctively, he had to have known she was a threat to his objective.

Was this still the case?

His hands lingered on her shoulder before leading her outside.

He'd never find another person like her. Despite everything, she'd not wavered from him in any way—not in her words, her feelings, or her intentions.

Her love for him had persisted, unconditionally.

His heart swelled.

Once the door to the carriage closed behind them, with her seated beside him on the front-facing bench, Jeremy wasn't quite ready to bid her goodnight yet.

"Is your Aunt Emma expecting you home at any

particular time? Or would you be amenable to driving around a while?"

She turned in surprise but nodded. "No. I mean, yes. I mean... No, she isn't expecting me and yes, I am quite amenable to your suggestion." She laughed. "It's a lovely night."

The air in his chest eased. He was making the right decision.

He lowered his hand between them and when she did the same, he entwined her fingers with his and squeezed gently.

Being with her had always been good for him. How had he managed so long without her?

He pounded on the ceiling using his cane and, after giving his driver new instructions through the small opening, closed the small sliding door and settled in beside her again.

"Quite a banner day." Lydia was the first to speak.

"My preparation paid off." Jeremy exhaled loudly, running his free hand through his hair. "It's why I haven't been able to take you to see the progress at the ware-house." It was the truth; he'd spent his every waking hour gathering documents and sorting through reports.

"I wasn't sure..."

"But I'm a fool. I should have made time for you." He released her hand and slid his arm behind her shoulders instead, turning at the same time so he could see her better. "How are you?"

Such a simple question, and one that usually had an obvious answer.

"The truth?" The mere fact that she'd ask him this was revealing enough.

"Ah, Lydia." She was so very precious to him—even more precious than before. "Tell me."

He felt the small tremor run through her and pulled her closer.

"I'm... hopeful. But also afraid."

He'd hurt her. But she had reason to hope again.

"Because of what happened between the two of us?"

She nodded slowly.

"Come here."

CHAPTER 11

*J*eremy didn't care that he was revisiting trouble when he drew her onto his lap. But having her weight settle atop him felt like the most natural thing in the world.

"Is it because of the vase?" he teased. "Because I'll have you know I've already located a replica that was made right here in London."

"You did? You are teasing me." But she was smiling now and sliding her hand up his chest and then onto his shoulder.

"You always give me reason to smile, did you know that?" Jeremy leaned his mouth very close to hers and then, tempted by the uptilt of her lips, closed the distance completely.

She welcomed his kiss with a soft sigh.

"Forgive me?"

"Always," she breathed in answer.

At first, the kiss was a tender dance of memories, apologies, and forgiveness. But when she wound her other hand around his neck and arched into him, Jeremy's heart raced, and he unbuttoned her coat with one hand while his other clutched her tightly against him.

"Jeremy." Her whispered sighs ignited an almost unnatural desire to please her.

With her coat unfastened, Jeremy dipped his hand inside and cupped her breast over the fabric of her gown.

His fingertips located the tops of her stays, and he trailed them along the edge. She was a lady. If he had any honor at all, he would have asked for her hand the day he'd kissed her in the warehouse, and then again at Heart Place.

If he had any honor at all, he would have begged her to be his wife the day she'd come to Galewick Manor after he'd stormed out of his meeting with her brothers.

Honor wasn't the simple concept he'd always believed it to be. Because the loyalty a man felt wasn't limited to one person. And if it was, it could become a trap.

Is that what honoring his brother's memory had become?

LYDIA MOVED to twist around on him, just as she had before, but this time, he held her in check.

"But..."

Jeremy cut off her delicate protest easily enough. "Let me," he whispered against her lips. "I want to touch you."

His hand abandoned her breast so he could gather her skirts in his fist, edging the hem up past her knee to where her stocking ended—stockings held in place by silk ribbons wrapped around each perfect thigh. He was glad the curtains on the window had been left open, allowing enough light from the moon to filter inside so he could fully appreciate those perfect thighs. Plump, pale, and tender. The blood thrumming through his veins felt like fire.

"I want to taste you." *Everywhere*. He plucked at one of the ribbons, and then dipped his hand between her legs, brushing the back of his fingers over skin that was more delicate than a butterfly's wings.

Her gaze, occasionally reflecting flashes of the moonlight, didn't waver from his. It was so very like her, not to shy away from her feelings or to question something that felt so natural and right.

He skimmed up that soft skin until to caress the petals at her opening. "You like this?" His own breathing sounded loud in his ears. She was wet and slick and willing.

"Yes." So straightforward. "I want…"

"What?"

"More."

Jeremy took only a moment to fondle her seam before extending his finger inside. "Like that?"

She licked her lips and nodded.

He didn't know what excited him more, touching her like this, or watching her while he did so. As he moved in and out, and then stretched her with a second finger, her breaths turned into gasps, and all the while, she gazed at him trustingly.

It felt more intimate than anything he'd ever done.

He drew lazy circles around velvety flesh and then explored higher.

"Jeremy!" she surrendered, closing her eyes and dropping her head backward.

There was so much wonder about her. Jeremy drank in the graceful length of her neck, her breasts heaving, the tip of her tongue as it reached just beyond the pearls of her teeth.

The carriage was turning, and the light from one of the street lanterns gave him a glimpse of his arm reaching between her legs. The sight amplified the throbbing in his cock, and he closed his eyes, willing her to reach around and—

He never quite finished that thought when the springs on the carriage suddenly sent the two of them flying.

His driver jerked the vehicle but had failed to avoid the large rut hidden by the darkness.

Holding Lydia on his lap, and both hands, er, occupied, Jeremy barely managed to cushion her fall as both of them were thrown to the floor.

The carriage came to a halt, and here they were again, him fully clothed and entirely too aroused for the circumstances. Or perhaps it was understandable.

Because once again she was straddling him, each leg bent at the knee along his hips and her center pressing down in such a way that was certain to lead to far greater improprieties.

"PARDON MY DRIVING, My Lord! My apologies to the Lady. Is everyone all right back there?" Lydia heard the driver's voice through the sliding door but when she went to speak, nothing came out.

"I believe so, Phillips. Are you hurt, Lydia?" Jeremy's voice sounded at the same time his body vibrated beneath her.

"No. No. I'm fine." At least her voice was functioning again.

"Would you like me to turn for Heart Place now, My Lord?"

Lydia went to move, but Jeremy's hands held fast to her hips. "Not quite yet. I'll let you know."

"Very good, My Lord." The small door slid closed then, and after a moment, with a gentle lurch, they were on the move again.

With no way to keep keep her balance, Lydia fell forward, dropping her hands onto Jeremy's shoulders. "You are my prisoner now," she teased. Because he could escape if he wanted to.

She knew he did not.

"Do you trust me, Lydia?"

Her eyes were adjusted to the darkness on the floor now, and she could almost make out his features. "Of course, I do," she answered softly. Despite everything, she would always trust him with her life.

But his next words gave her pause.

"Walk forward on your knees." He was still holding her hips but was now urging her to move. "Grab the straps by the window." She already knew he was aroused by their position, in fact, she was becoming quite educated as to this particular phenomenon. Then why? "And hold onto them tightly."

He was gathering her skirts again, pushing them up and urging her higher, toward his...

But if she kept inching forward like this...

His hands on her bare thighs kept her moving, and then lifted her.

If the rocking of the carriage hadn't sent her hands suddenly grasping for the straps, the sensation of Jeremy's whiskers along her inner thigh would have done so.

Gripping them, she went to pull herself up.

"Trust me?" His words drifted up from beneath her skirts at the same time the heat of his breath warmed the place between her legs.

Where she knew she was wet from moments before.

"I do but— Ah... ah..." She squeezed the leather straps when intense pleasure shocked her into acquiescence. "You shouldn't! Oh, good heavens! Jeremy!" She nearly melted when she felt his jaw graze over her apex followed by a hot, wet stroke of his tongue.

Except he chose that moment to pause. "Shall I continue?" His voice vibrated her insides intimately.

"Um... Please?" This.

It felt too good.

He couldn't stop now. She would die. She would simply die!

He chuckled beneath her, and Lydia jumped.

"Come back here."

"I'm not going anywhere." With the side of her face pressed against the cool glass of the window, she was determined not to fall apart. He'd said he wanted to taste her, but she'd had no idea he'd meant—she simply had had no idea.

The same feelings she'd had when they broke the vase were building steadily again. And then not so steadily. Because with each stroke and thrust he made below her, she pictured him there. His tongue. The whiskers along his jaw. The image itself was enough—

"Yessssss!" Hot and cold lightning shot through her veins. The leather slipped through her fingers as sharp pleasure took hold and she all but collapsed, trying to move off him while mumbling an incoherent apology.

"I've got you, love," he answered beneath her skirts, adding something that sounded like, "and I'm never letting you go." But she couldn't be certain.

When she finally discovered her muscles again, she squirmed, and he assisted her down to lay beside him.

The carriage wasn't all that wide, forcing him to bend his legs up and her to lay half on top of his chest, one leg thrown over his waist.

She wasn't the slightest bit uncomfortable. Not even when he turned to claim her mouth, and she tasted herself in his kiss. Being with him was... It was wonderful.

"That was... unexpected." She had to say something. They couldn't roll around Mayfair all night, after all.

"I've been imagining that for three days now."

"You haven't!"

"Planned this very scenario."

He'd provided her with glimpses of this side of himself before—with a dry joke or a secret grin. And each time, she'd tumbled even deeper into love.

Trouble was, now that she'd experienced him this

way, she wasn't at all certain she could ever let go again. And yet she might not have a choice.

He might love her, but would it be enough for him to get over whatever had caused him to push her away to begin with?

"Sleepy?" He held her tucked against him in a way that partially dispelled some of her concerns.

"Hmm..." Lydia hummed in contentment, memorizing his cedary scent so she could summon it when they were apart. "You must be exhausted though."

He laughed. "It was a good day. But I suppose I ought to take you home." He shifted both of them off the floor and onto the bench and kissed the top of her head. "Allow me to correct that. Today was much better than good. It was practically perfect."

Lydia wondered if her maid would think she looked like the cat who ate the canary when she came in. Feeling daring, she reached her hand across to his lap.

"I know precisely what you need."

When he grasped her wrist and stilled her hand over his straining member, she realized she'd guessed rightly.

"We'll have time enough in the future to... ahem, address my situation properly. In the meantime—" Jeremy turned and caught her up in an almost desperate embrace just as the carriage pulled to a stop outside of Heart Place. Knowing they had only a few moments before the footman would open the door, he pulled back, breathing heavily.

"I have mountains of work waiting for me tomorrow," he all but growled. "But I miss you already."

"It can wait a day, can it not?"

"Minx." He brushed the side of her mouth with his thumb. "Come with me to visit the warehouse in the afternoon?"

Even shrouded in darkness, there was no missing the light of hope in his eyes.

"Yes." She didn't even hesitate.

CHAPTER 12

*L*ydia sat up and stretched with a giant yawn. It had taken her hours to fall asleep. Not that she'd never had trouble sleeping before, but this time, it had not been worries that kept her awake. It had been the memory of unimaginable intimacy, pleasure, and rightness.

And most of all, the tantalizing words spoken inside a dark carriage. *We'll have time enough in the future...*

Those words alluded to a promise.

Louise drew the curtains back, and a dreary drizzling sky begrudgingly allowed gray light to filter inside. Clucking her tongue, her maid held up a gown and brushed at the skirt. "The periwinkle today or the mauve?"

"The periwinkle," Lydia answered. "But I'm going to the docks later and will need to change into something drab."

Lydia wished she could dress her best for him today,

but it would not be wise to show up on the docks looking even more out of place than she already did.

Even though she knew he would like the periwinkle on her.

Lydia lowered herself on to the vanity bench and stared into the mirror. Did she look different today? So much had happened, so much had changed. She leaned closer, touching her cheek.

Her eyes seemed to twinkle more than usual, and her lips looked slightly swollen. Would Clarissa notice any changes the next time she saw her? Lydia bit her lip.

Luckily, Lucas and Blackheart weren't here. Lucas, even more so than Lucinda, had always had an uncanny ability to guess her secrets.

"Has my aunt broken her fast yet this morning?"

"Not yet, My Lady." Louise dragged the brush through Lydia's long wavy lengths. "This hair of yours could use a trim." She then twisted it into a neat chignon, leaving a few tendrils to soften Lydia's face.

"I like this style," Lydia commented. "But I think you're right. Especially when this weather warms up."

"*If* it warms up," Louise said. "I, for one, am ready for some sunshine."

"I will not argue on that point."

What remained of the morning passed slowly. Lydia enjoyed a leisurely breakfast with Aunt Emma, hearing all about the salon she and Lord Beasley had attended the night before and even raising her brows at a few suspected scandals that might be brewing.

Once her aunt was settled into the drawing room with a book and her knitting, Lydia met with her brother's cook, and then the housekeeper, performing a few tasks that Blackheart's Duchess would eventually take on fully. For the most part, the staff functioned autonomously when Blackheart was not in town.

Just as she and Mrs. Duckworth finished locking away the silver, Mr. Hill appeared in the doorway.

"A Mrs. Mumford here to see you, My Lady."

Lydia had to think a moment before she could place the name. What was Ollie's governess doing coming here?

"Why on earth?" And then it dawned on her that something must be wrong. "Where is she?"

"I've asked her to wait in the north drawing room."

Not taking time to untie her apron, Lydia rushed from the dining room toward the front of the house where she found the governess pacing back and forth and wringing her hands.

"What's happened?" Lydia didn't bother wasting time with niceties.

"Master Oliver is missing, My Lady. A short while ago, I found him outside in the garden with two older boys. They were obviously from the docks, and His Lordship has made it very clear the child wasn't to associate with them. Mrs. Crone, of course, shooed them away. I thought nothing was amiss when Master Oliver returned without argument to the nursery, but I went to check on the nuncheon, and he was gone when I came back. We've turned the entire house upside down looking for him, and Lady Tempest says good riddance, but I'm worried. Those boys..." Mrs. Mumford paused long enough to shudder. "They're trouble. And Oliver was doing so well."

"Did you send for Lord Tempest?"

"We have, but he isn't in his offices."

Lydia refused to panic. "Sit down. We'll find him. Ollie will be fine."

Lydia set her mind immediately to contemplating various scenarios. "Lord Tempest must be at the warehouse." Or perhaps the offices of the new company he'd purchased.

But Lydia wasn't willing to sit around waiting for a servant to locate him. If these little thieves and thugs knew where Ollie had been living, they might also know that his new guardian was the same man who was making trouble for the gang bosses.

Ollie had hidden in the warehouse once before. It was likely he'd do so again. It was possible that he'd already found Jeremy himself.

Lydia burst to her feet again. "Return to Lord Tempest's residence and wait there in case Ollie returns on his own." Perhaps Ollie was just being curious. That was possible but...

"I'll go to the warehouse myself and send word as soon as I've found him." She ushered the governess out the front door and, at Mr. Hill's startled expression, relayed the situation. She needed a carriage right away, and her coat. She wouldn't take time to change.

"A carriage was scheduled for your aunt, but you can take it instead. And Reginald and Trevor are coming along." Mr. Hill didn't ask if she wished to have the manservants go with her, he simply told her this.

Already thinking of all the places Ollie might be hiding, she simply nodded, eager to get to the warehouse.

"Very well, but we must hurry!" She slid her arms into her coat and then pulled on her gloves, moving anxiously toward the door as she did so. So far, luck appeared to be on her side as the carriage pulled up almost immediately after she'd stepped outside.

"The Tuesday warehouse, John!" she shouted up. "And hurry, please!"

Because a small boy's life might be at stake!

She was barely aware of the two footmen hopping onto the back as the carriage pulled into the street and turned toward East London.

If she didn't locate Ollie right away at the warehouse, she'd drive straight to the shipping company's office to alert Jeremy. She wasn't precisely sure where it was located, but surely, John would know? Oh, dear, what would she do if he didn't? The last thing she wanted was to drive around aimlessly in search of him while poor little Ollie...

She halted that train of thought. Dwelling on worst case scenarios had never been something she'd practiced.

He's fine. He has to be fine. Ollie was likely hiding somewhere in the warehouse—or better yet, in Jeremy's townhouse.

Not until they turned onto Wapping Street did she stop to remember the promise she'd made to Jeremy about coming there alone. But she did have two manservants with her. And her driver.

And this was an emergency!

When they pulled to a halt, Reginald barely managed

to lower the step before she jumped down to the road. "If he's not inside, we'll need to go to Ludwig Bros. Shipping. Do you know where that is?"

Her coachman shook his head and looked back questioningly toward the two manservants. Of course, why would two footmen who'd spent most of their time working in Mayfair know where a shipping company's offices might be?

It wasn't fair but she couldn't keep her irritation out of her voice.

"See what you can find out. I'll be out in a moment." Hearing the construction inside, she was hopeful she would find Ollie safely chatting with one of the workmen. "Someone around here must know where it is!"

The door swung open easily this time, and she noticed that the lock had been repaired. As she entered, sounds of construction grew louder.

One of the workers approached her almost instantly. "I'm sorry, ma'am, you can't come in here. A lady like yourself oughtn't be down here anyway."

"I'm Lady Lydia Cockfield, and I am one of the directors of this project." She really did not have time for this. "But I'm looking for a young boy, about so high, dark hair and violet eyes. Have you seen him?"

He turned away from her without answering. "Hey, Nick! Any violet-eyed urchins around here today?" He half-laughed until the other man pointed toward one of the backdoors.

"Went outside!"

"Thank you," Lydia called.

"Lady, you really don't want to be walking around out there. Why don't you go to Lord Tempest's office?"

"I'll only be a moment." Lydia pushed her way past the man acting as a guard, despite his protests behind her. "Ollie?" she shouted over the din just in case he was hiding inside somewhere.

When she arrived at the door that led outside, she was pleased to find it already open. Some of the debris left-over from the days when the warehouse had been in operation had been removed, but an indescribable stench remained.

"Ollie!"

She tiptoed over a few puddles, skirting around mounds of rubbish, and had almost given up when she caught a flash of movement out of the corner of her eye.

"Ollie!" She increased her pace, grimacing when her foot landed in some of the foul-smelling water.

When she rounded the corner, the sight that met her eyes sucked the breath out of her. Robbed of his jacket, Ollie was hunched over, clutching his stomach and moaning while a larger boy had hold of the back of his shirt.

Lydia approached and Ollie glanced up, face bloodied, with pleading eyes. "Go back!" he shouted.

But of course, she couldn't leave him like this! "What on earth is going on here?"

"Go on!" Panic entered his eyes.

What had they done to him?

"Leave this child alone!" she ordered, rushing forward.

"I wouldn't if I was you." Steel-like arms caught her

from behind before she'd taken more than a few steps. "This 'er? This the lady tha' was wif Tempest?"

The other boy—the one who, with the same violet eyes, couldn't be anyone other than Ollie's brother—jerked at Ollie and glanced up.

"It ain't her!" Ollie answered.

"Shut up, ya little liar," Buck snarled at Ollie before glancing back to whoever had a hold of Lydia. "Yeah, but why would we wanna mess wif 'er?"

"Help m-mph!" Lydia barely managed to shout before the villain holding her captive smothered her mouth with his foul-smelling hand. In response, she squirmed and fought with all her might to twist away. When she tried to bite him, he pinched her lips together with his fingers. He seemed rather experienced at this sort of treachery.

"Hold still, ya bloomin' wench." His arm tightened, almost vicelike. Fighting like this wasn't going to do her any good, and what little she'd done already had left her struggling to draw air in through her nose.

"If this 'ere is Tempest's woman, Farley might find her useful in gettin' back at 'im."

"She ain't though." Ollie jerked out of Buck's hold. "She's jus' one o' the birds buildin' the orphanage. She ain't gonna be no use to Farley. He'll just be mad at ya for messing with one o' the nobs."

Ollie was trying to protect her. For the first time since she'd been coming to the docks, genuine fear swept through her.

Would one of the workmen come looking for her? She ought to have brought Reginald or Trevor along for protection. She'd been far too confident for her own good.

But she wasn't ready to give up yet. Even if the workmen failed to come looking for her, her brother's servants would. But would they come quickly enough?

"Farley needs bait to get to Tempest." The voice near her ear was almost gleeful.

"Then what are we waitin' for?"

"Knock 'er out, will ya? She's tryin' to bite me and we can't exactly carry 'er through the streets screaming an' 'ollerin', now can we?"

Buck moved forward, flexing his fist, and Lydia realized that, for the first time in her life, she was going to be hit by another person. Terrified, she renewed her squirming and twisting and even managed to land a kick on the blighter behind her, but it was no use.

The last thing she saw was a bloodied wrist flying toward her face. Her last thought was that Reginald and Trevor were not going to come in time to save her.

And her last feeling was fear, not for herself, but for Ollie and Jeremy.

And then everything turned black.

CHAPTER 13

"The bastard no doubt took for granted these records wouldn't survive down here." Baxter grimaced and then let out a low whistle. "How could Rudolph not have realized what his brother was up to?"

"Rudolph never would have sold if he had."

Jeremy carefully examined a faded record and then tossed it aside. He'd suspected the records might be in Ludwig's half flooded basements but hadn't expected this.

Each mildew-ridden box required meticulous care while opening; the first one having practically fallen apart in his hands when he'd moved to carry it to the offices upstairs.

He flicked his gaze around the soggy basement. Considering the waterlines on the walls, as well as the bog-like floor, it was a wonder any records remained intact.

That was why they were opening them in place and

documenting items of significance in the shadowy lights of a few lanterns.

He, Baxter, and a few of his clerks had been at it for hours and an alarming pattern was beginning to emerge. With Arthur on the front line, Jeremy had followed the progress of both sides diligently, religiously even, and each cluster of losses Ludwig Bros. incurred, had preceded unprecedented enemy victories. The timeline of events was too uncanny to be a coincidence.

"So they were paid by the government to ship them and then took a second payment after handing supplies over to the insurgents." Baxter shook his head. "Here's more payments from Leo to Farley." He set the receipt on an increasingly growing pile. Periodically, one of Jeremy's trusted clerks would climb down the rickety steps to transport them upstairs.

With each receipt found that didn't list Arthur's name, Jeremy was that much closer to his goal. He rubbed the back of his neck and carefully extracted another file just as the door at the top of the narrow stairway opened and closed. Rather than his clerk's etched and tired-looking face, however, Lord Westerley appeared.

He and his countess, as importers of American Whiskey, were very interested in wiping the docks clean of the current gang activity, and last night, the earl had offered up any assistance he could provide.

"Damn, Tempest. I thought you'd be out by now." Westerley had to bend over in order to avoid the overhead joists as he moved deeper into the dungeon-like room. "Why don't you just have them brought upstairs?"

In answer, Baxter lifted the corner of one of his rejected receipts, which promptly tore in two. "They might not make the trip that way."

Jeremy glanced at his time piece. He was going to have to send word to Lydia that he couldn't escort her to the warehouse today. He could not leave this task unfinished. They were over halfway through the boxes and he'd not yet found any evidence that Arthur had been involved.

All would be settled by tomorrow. And then he could ask her that all important question. She would understand.

Jeremy cast off the receipt in his hand and took up another. It was dated almost two years ago, April 12th, 1828, and listed names that had become quite familiar to him by now. But there was a smudged one that he had not seen on any of the others.

Jeremy lifted it closer to his eyes and squinted. His heart sank.

$\sim$

COMING AWAKE, Lydia opened her eyes and saw... nothing. Was this a nightmare? She was blindfolded!

And her hands were bound!

Familiar sounds, that of a bell ringing, distant voices, and water splashing against the pier hinted that she was somewhere on the docks. A most pungent scent of tar, fish and filth confirmed her guess.

The memory came rushing back to her of Ollie, and his brother, and the person who'd grabbed her from

136

behind. She licked her lips and was thankful that whoever was keeping her captive had at least removed the gag.

A sensation of motion, of rocking softly, gave away that she must be on one of the abandoned ships. It had to be where the gang bosses were hiding.

How long had she been here? Hours? A day?

Had only one night passed since she'd been sitting down to a lovely dinner with Mayfair's elite?

"Hello?" She tested her voice, even though she was fairly certain she was alone. It came out little more than a croak. "Can I have some water, please?" She waited, half afraid someone would answer her, but also half afraid that no one would.

She was a woman who had been captured by unscrupulous individuals. Never had she been so aware of her own powerlessness. Never had she felt so vulnerable.

A few minutes later, she heard a door open, and light filtered through the fabric covering her eyes.

"'Ere." A cup was pressed to her lips, and she had no choice but to tilt her head and swallow, spilling a good deal of the water in the process.

It dribbled down her chin, onto her chest, and then gown. She was no longer wearing her coat. Someone had taken it off of her while she'd been unconscious.

She shivered, not daring to allow herself to think about that.

"Are you Ollie's brother, Buck?" She lifted her chin as though she could sense where he was. There had to be some goodness in him if he was Ollie's brother.

"What's it to ya?"

"Where's Ollie, is he all right?" She hadn't been able to save him. In fact, she'd made matters worse. But she couldn't focus on that right now.

"He needs to learn 'is place," the boy grunted.

"Why are you keeping me here? You should let me go before you end up in even more trouble than you're already in."

"Ha," he scoffed, but then lifted the drink to her mouth again. A breeze landed on her face and Buck turned away before she could attempt another sip.

"She's the one, ain't she?" Ollie's brother asked whoever had entered.

"So pretty. Maybe we won't have to off her." Cold, rough hands grabbed ahold of hers. "We need to untie her though, so she can sign the note. Won't do any good if Tempest doesn't believe we have her." The loosening around her wrists brought relief but as she realized their intentions, fear shot through her like a knife.

They were going to ransom her. But for what?

"You gonna kill the Earl o'Tempest, Farley? He right deserves it, for all the trouble he's makin'."

And then something hard and cold pressed against her forehead. Not having seen it, nor ever having held one, she knew instinctively that this despicable person was threatening her with a pistol.

"When that meddling nob shows up, Buck, I'm gonna shoot him—" He jammed the barrel into her head with even more force. "Right." He pushed harder. "Between. The eyes." He made a shooting sound with his mouth and then chuckled.

She stopped breathing even though he'd said he wasn't going to kill her. But he meant to kill Jeremy!

She couldn't allow that to happen. She'd rather die herself.

She'd been so stupid to go outside alone!

The person named Farley removed the gun from her head. But this only provided temporary relief. Buck was laughing as he moved behind her. He loosened the blindfold and then allowed it to drop.

Light coming through the open door beat onto her pupils almost as though she was staring into the sun. But she blinked and forced herself to stare down at the floor. Light meant freedom couldn't be too far away.

And with the door open, the dock sounds were louder. With watering eyes, she focused on her hands, unbound now, and flexed them in her lap.

"We're gonna need you to write a sweet letter begging your lover to save you." Farley thrust a pencil into her hand.

More laughter from Buck, and she glanced up. Farley wasn't as young as she'd thought he would be. But perhaps just as living on the docks had caused Ollie to look younger, it had aged Farley prematurely.

She hovered the tip of the pencil over the blank sheet of paper, but as she went to write, Ollie's brother asked Farley a question that sent various facts clicking around in her brain.

"Is he really Arthur's brother?"

Were they talking about Jeremy?

Arthur Gilcrest had been captured in an ambush. An ambush where a fortune's worth of ammunition had been stolen. The facts weren't only clicking, but sparking and shooting now.

"That he is. Got a right long stick up his arse though."

And Lucas had been Arthur's commanding officer. Since he'd returned from the front, he'd been investigating the ambush and must have found something suspicious.

Sitting and listening to Buch and Farley discussing Jeremy's brother was providing answers to the questions that had taunted her for months.

The day Jeremy came to offer for her, Lucas must have told Jeremy he suspected Arthur was a traitor.

That day, when she'd told him that Ollie shouldn't have to turn his back on his brother, Jeremy had said... *That's why...* But then he'd stopped. He'd told her he'd never wanted her to have to decide, that it wouldn't have been fair. She'd been half-right to guess that Jeremy had not wanted her to have to turn her back on her brothers. But the choice wouldn't have been between her brothers and herself. It would have been between her brothers and *Jeremy*.

Jeremy hadn't wanted her to have to choose between her family and the man she loved. That was why...

Oh Jeremy!

Arthur had always been Jeremy's weak spot. And when faced with something so contemptable as the accusation that Arthur had betrayed his own countrymen, Jeremy hadn't been able to believe it.

Lydia nearly sobbed as she grasped the truth. The purchase of Ludwig Shipping hadn't been about cleaning up the docks at all. It had been all about clearing his brother's name.

And that was not going to happen. Because Arthur had been a traitor.

"What are you waiting for?" Farley nudged her arm, his foul breath nearly making her gag. She shook her head.

Lydia's realization had left her stunned and unable to think about anything else.

"I… I don't know what to write." The sound of her own voice jolted her back to the present.

A plan. She needed a plan and in order to come up with one, she needed to keep her wits about her.

Farley drew up a chair and sat down, crossing his legs and lounging in a manner that ought to be far too relaxed for the situation.

"To my Darling Earl of Tempest," he dictated and then dropped his foot and leaned forward. "Go on, now. Write it."

She did just that, in flowery, looping letters. She realized as he watched her that he couldn't make out her words.

He was uneducated and if he did know how to read, he'd only have comprehension of the most rudimentary of letters.

"Now what?" she asked innocently.

"If you wanna see me alive again, you go to the Tuesday warehouse at sunset tonight. Alone. If ya do anything stupid, they'll kill me." And then he sniggered. "If ya ever wan' another taste o' me you best do what they want. And sign it, yer loving lady."

Lydia wrote instead: *I'm being held captive on one of the abandoned ships near the broken pier. Farley and his men will be waiting for you at the warehouse at sunset but that's a trap. He wants to kill you. Please be careful and if anything happens to me, know that I've always loved you. Yours forever, Lydia.*

Feeling hesitant, and a little concerned that Farley could read it after all, she glanced up. "Anything else?"

"Na, just fold it up and seal it with a kiss." He waved his gun in the air, laughing.

Lydia did precisely that and handed it over.

"Noah!" he shouted out the door and an older version of Buck appeared in the opening. "Make sure this gits to Tempest. An' don't ya let no one follow you."

She breathed a sigh of relief when Noah tucked the note into his shirt and disappeared. And another when Farley handed the gun to Buck.

"Take this." With his hands free, Farley then grasped tight hold of her wrists and tied her hands in front of her again. "If she does anything stupid, shoot her. But not in the head or the body. She's more use to us if she's alive for now. If anyone else comes, though. Shoot them in the head."

"Not the heart?" Buck asked.

"Wherever." Farley sent Buck an annoyed look over his shoulder. "Just be sure they end up swimmin' with the fishes."

"Understood, boss."

Farley strode toward the door and then halted, jerking around to pin his gaze on her. "You nobs should have minded yer own business."

She wanted nothing more than to scream back at

him. Because when the thieves had begun stealing the soldiers' supplies, they'd put the entire country in danger, making it everyone's business.

"How did you get Arthur to do it?" she asked instead.

"Bought 'his vowels, how else? Every man has his weakness. Funny thing is, Tempest's little brother wasn't loyal to no one. Fickle as 'ell, he was." And with that, Farley stepped outside and closed the door behind him, leaving her alone with Buck again.

With Buck and the gun.

Lydia exhaled a slow breath. If Arthur hadn't been loyal to Farley, it meant he'd regretted his actions at some point. That had to mean something.

She glanced over at Buck, who was staring down the barrel of the pistol as though trying to comprehend how it worked.

Perhaps knowing Arthur had been coerced into his treachery would help Jeremy reconcile himself to it. She only hoped she'd stay alive long enough to tell him.

CHAPTER 14

"I hate to interrupt, but I think we might have a problem." Westerley's tone was serious enough that it demanded Jeremy's unfettered attention.

"On the docks?" Jeremy glanced up, feeling the walls of the basement suddenly closing in around him.

Westerly nodded. "Word's out that you intend to clean house. We knew they'd fight back, but something's brewing around the old ship we believe to be their headquarters."

Baxter turned to Jeremy. "We can't delay the raid, not unless we're willing to risk the whole lot of them getting away."

"Agreed. The gang bosses would only set up somewhere else."

The club owner was already rising from the crate where he'd been seated. "I'll send word to my men."

Sounds of more descending footsteps echoed in the room and this time, it was one of Jeremy's clerks, Smithy, who came into view. But he was not alone.

The very last person Jeremy wanted or expected to see in the dimly lit basement appeared behind him, a man he'd once considered practically a brother. Jeremy narrowed his eyes at Blackheart.

With hawkish features and hair so dark it was almost black, even in a dingy and foul-smelling cellar, the duke managed to exude the arrogance that had been bred into him.

"What the hell are you doing here, Blackheart?" Jeremy stretched to see around this unwanted visitor, but apparently, he'd come alone. "Lucas isn't with you?"

Lydia's brother held up both hands, chuckling softly. "I come in peace." He glanced around with a sardonic lift of his brow. "And felicitations on a most interesting acquisition."

Jeremy inhaled deeply and then glanced down at his fob watch again. This day, it seemed, wasn't going at all as planned. When he failed to show at Heart Place to collect her, would she think he was avoiding her again?

"Not necessary," he answered dismissively. He needed someone to tell Lydia he wasn't coming. He fisted his hands.

"Ah, but it is." Blackheart stepped further into the room, his boots making a squishing sound as he did so. "Lucas is backing down. And seeing as you're in a war of sorts, and we're all on the same side, I've come to offer our support. Whatever you need. If it's within the realm of my capabilities, I'll provide it."

Jeremy paused. As much as he wanted to, he was in no position to refuse Blackheart's offer of help. This was no longer just about him. It was about protecting not only an orphanage or the docks but England itself.

He glanced down at the incriminating receipt in his hand and swallowed hard, practically choking on his shame.

"You were right." Jeremy forced himself to look up into Blackheart's eyes. "Arthur's betrayal wasn't limited to his family, or his wife, or his brother." In that moment it felt as though his heart turned into a void as dark as this basement. It was over. "He betrayed Lucas that day." Not only Lucas, but every man whose life had been on the line. He'd been the reason five of them had died.

"Arthur was a traitor." Jeremy said.

Arthur had betrayed his country. The truth echoed in his head like a death knoll but then completed the puzzle perfectly. *His brother had committed treason.*

Jeremy had not wanted to believe it. But he'd known. Somehow deep in his heart he had known.

His own blood…

"He was." Blackheart didn't blink as he stood there and agreed with him. "I'm sorry, Temp."

Jeremy dragged his gaze around the dank room where he'd so badly wanted to discover evidence that would exculpate Arthur. He had needed that proof.

He'd needed it to silence his own suspicions.

Defeated, he ran a hand through his hair. He'd been a fool—an idiot. Where did he go from here? His family name, the title his sons would one day inherit, would be forever blackened.

"Lucas spoke with the general, and they've decided to

keep the records sealed. In fact if word was to get out, he says it could harm the effort."

Jeremy nodded, feeling dead inside. "It's not exactly fair to the families of the soldiers who didn't make it home."

"War isn't fair," Blackheart said.

But footsteps thundering overhead had both men suddenly glancing up, then over to the stairway where another one of Jeremy's clerks appeared with, of all people, Ollie at his side. And Ollie looked to have gotten into trouble again. Even worse this time if the swelling around his eyes was anything to go by.

"M'lord!" Ollie ran heedlessly toward him, knocking one of the boxes into the mud in the process. "They've got her! You 'ave ta save her!"

"They've got who, Ollie?" Jeremy edged the boy closer.

"They've got Lady Liddy."

His blood turned to ice. With Ollie's words, thoughts of Arthur all but vanished.

"This was delivered just moments ago." Smithy handed over a folded note with Jeremy's name written in flowery writing.

"They said they was gonna use her as insurance. An' I'm not sure wot that is but it didn't sound good."

Jeremy opened the note, and as he read the contents, a roaring sounded in his ears. He looked up from it and met Blackheart's solemn gaze. "They have Lydia."

. . .

BLACKHEART, Baxter, and Westerley said they needed thirty minutes to round up the men who were prepared to raid the gang bosses' hideout. While they did that, Jeremy followed Ollie along the wharf to the ship where they were keeping Lydia.

Watching the gang members carrying stolen ammunition onto the abandoned ship, as though they were barrels of fish, Jeremy required every ounce of patience not to rush inside to save her.

He also had to convince Ollie, who knew the layout of the ship and wanted to go inside and check on Lydia, that it was best to wait as well. The sun was nearly set, and they'd have the cloak of darkness in a matter of minutes.

"It's all my fault," Ollie whispered, even though the two of them were far enough away not to be overheard. "Buck said he needed my help. But it was a lie. Buck didn't like that I was staying at yer big fancy 'ouse. Do you think 'e could stay with you too? He's not so bad, really. And he's my brother."

Jeremy kept his gaze pinned on the window where Ollie said they were keeping Lydia. Two guards watched the boarding plank and at least a dozen were manning the pier, a few of them carrying lanterns. He could almost imagine himself being successful going in on his own, but there were too damned many of them—all ages too. It sickened him to see boys who looked younger than Ollie milling about on what ought to have been a deserted wreck.

"I don't know, Ollie. Let's save Lady Lydia first." But he wasn't immune to the turmoil Ollie was feeling—the desire to protect a brother.

Patting the pistol in his jacket, he glanced over his shoulder, sensing Baxter's men moving into place.

If he heard any indication of Lydia's distress, he'd go in guns blazing, alone or not. In her note to him, she'd told him she'd always loved him. That she was his forever.

A pain stabbed his heart, making it difficult to draw in his next breath.

No one else in the world made him feel the way she did. She could make him laugh when the world seemed humorless. She provided hope when his future felt hopeless.

He'd been a damned fool to ever walk away from her. If something happened to her, he could never forgive himself.

Hearing quiet footsteps approaching behind him, Jeremy stiffened. But he breathed a sigh of relief when he saw that it was only Blackheart.

It was time.

"Everyone's in place." Blackheart crouched down beside him. He'd known the duke for years, but he didn't think he'd ever seen such a bleak expression in the man's eyes. Lydia's brother must have seen a similar expression on his own face, because he added, "We'll save her."

"We will," Jeremy agreed grimly.

"And then you and I will talk."

Jeremy only nodded at this. A brilliant light flashed off to the left, the predetermined signal giving him the go-ahead to move in.

The men that had been assembled overtook the

guards on the dock within less than thirty seconds, the men on the rooftops in even less time.

Jeremy didn't bother with the plank but sprinted past it, to the opposite end of the ship where Ollie said they were keeping her. He then used the momentum provided by his speed to leap across the water to the ship's deck. Blackheart was only a few steps behind him, landing almost silently a split second later.

"She's in the cabin on the quarterdeck." Jeremy pointed to the window Ollie had shown him. He and Blackheart no longer bothered with keeping silent since the gang was well aware of their presence by now. With each pistol shot that sounded, his heart skipped a beat.

The door where Lydia was being kept was unguarded now. He tried the handle, but it was locked.

Jeremy glanced toward Blackheart and with a giant rush of adrenaline, kicked the door in, sending it not only flying open but also knocking it partially off its hinges.

His gaze found her immediately, tucked in the back of the shadowed room. Her hands were bound and she was gagged, with blood crusted on her face. An older looking boy was grasping her arm with one hand and holding a gun pointed directly at Jeremy's head with the other.

But Lydia was alive, and he fully intended she'd stay that way.

"Put the gun down," Blackheart ordered in a voice that sounded deadly and quiet as he moved to stand beside Jeremy.

"Mmmmph!" Lydia stared back at him—not with terror—but with trust and relief.

A deadly calm came on him, ironically at the same time, white anger anchored his purpose. Whoever had made her bleed would die for this.

Jeremy forced his gaze back to Buck—the same boy he'd caught sneaking into his garden more than once.

"Take yourself off, Tempest," the adolescent growled, waving the gun. "You may 'ave tricked my kid brother into goin' soft, but you ain't about to trick me."

"So." Jeremy forced himself to appear relaxed, slumping his shoulders and leaning against the door frame. "You call feeding him, giving him a warm bed, and providing him with an education 'tricking' him?" He allowed a disparaging grin to stretch his lips.

"Yer makin' him soft. So when you throw him back on the streets, he won't know how to take care of himself. At least Farley teaches everyone how to keep fed… and alive."

"But I've no intention of throwing Ollie out. And if you make the right decision, I'll give you a better life too." Jeremy was sincere. He'd told Ollie that Buck was trouble, but the boy could show him otherwise today. "Hot food. A warm bed every night."

Both he and Blackheart had managed to sidle into the room by now.

"It's your choice. All you need to do is drop the gun and I'll take you in, the same as your brother. This is the chance for you to have a meaningful life, Buck."

"And there's chocolates, Buck." Jeremy hadn't realized Ollie had come up on them, but now he stood in the door, his eyes filled with a sort of sacrificing love Jeremy knew all too well, pleading with his brother to make the right decision. "Mrs. Crump has all kinds and she's not stingy with 'em. Just let M'lady go. Please Buck?"

Buck tilted his head. He hadn't given Ollie an answer, but he relaxed the hand holding up the gun just enough to provide Jeremy and Blackheart with the opportunity they needed.

Jeremy met Lydia's gaze and as though she understood his silent instructions perfectly, she threw herself onto the floor the instant he and her brother pounced.

Buck was tough and wily though, and he wasn't about to go down without a fight. He kicked out and tried to throw a punch, but his efforts were in vain. It was two against one—two grown men against one boy.

The blast of the gun going off reverberated in Jeremy's ears as Buck made his choice. Blood splattered everywhere. Jeremy felt it on his hands, on his face, and he even tasted the coppery liquid in his mouth. He dropped to his knees, cursing, searching for the source and terrified that the blood might be Lydia's.

STRONG ARMS PULLED Lydia off the floor and then wrapped around her almost desperately.

"Are you hurt?" Jeremy removed the gag from her mouth and frantically ran his hands down her arms as though searching for the lost bullet. "Love? Are you all right?"

"I'm fine." It was all she could think to say. "I'm fine." She'd been terrified that he'd gone to the warehouse despite her letter, that he had somehow fallen into

Farley's trap. Feeling him whole and solid beside her brought so much relief that she burst into tears.

Eyes closed, face pressed against his chest, she forgot they were alone until she heard the sound of a flint strike from across the room.

She jerked her head up to make sure she hadn't imagined him, and sure as she lived, her brother stood staring down at the two of them. With a grimace, he flicked his gaze to the young man lying on the floor.

"It exploded in his hand." Blackheart lowered to his haunches, untying his cravat while Jeremy freed her wrists. "Bullet never made it out of the gun."

"Buck!" Ollie sprang across the room and dropped to his brother's side as well.

"Don't die, Buck!" Ollie's voice rose in panic. Lydia had never seen so much blood in her entire life.

Lord Westerley peered inside just then. "Everything under control in here? We're clear on deck. Farley's in Baxter's custody, and most of the others have been rounded up by the runners." He pointed to Buck. "What about this one?"

"I'll handle him." Blackheart glanced over at Jeremy, who nodded, and without another word, lifted Lydia into his arms.

"I'm getting her out now in case there's any more trouble."

"Good thinking." her brother agreed.

"But—" she sputtered. What about Ollie? "Don't I get a say?" she asked.

"No," both Jeremy and her brother answered in unison.

Well, then.

"Ollie?" Jeremy moved toward the door, adjusting his grip as he cradled her in his arms. "Are you coming with us?"

But Ollie didn't move. "What about Buck?" His violet eyes swam with tears.

"This one needs a doctor." Blackheart answered. "I'll drop the younger one at your townhouse after." Her brother didn't look up as he spoke, all of his attention focused on Buck's hand—what was left of it.

Jeremy turned to go, but Lydia stopped him by reaching out and catching the side of the door.

"Ollie?"

Her little orphan lifted his gaze to meet hers.

"I'm proud of you," she said. She needed him to know he wasn't to blame. *This was the bad people's fault.*

"I'm sorry," he said. "I got you caught."

"But you also helped save me." Lydia said with as much force as she could muster. "Do you understand?"

Ollie stared at her and then slowly nodded.

"This man—" Lydia pointed a Blackheart "—is my brother. He'll take care of you and Buck. Do as he says. All right?"

"Yes, M'Lady."

Lydia nodded and, suddenly too exhausted for any more words, buried her face in Jeremy's chest again. As he carried her off the ship and onto the wharf, she didn't look up once as approving voices thanked and congratulated him. He may not have set out to become a hero, but he'd become one, just the same.

And this didn't surprise Lydia at all.

CHAPTER 15

"*A*re you going to carry me all the way to Mayfair?" Lydia asked after they were some distance away from all of the excitement and activity on the ship.

"My carriage is at my office." He was a little out of breath by now.

Studying his profile in the moonlight, Lydia winced. "Are you angry with me?"

"Livid."

She wasn't sure if his short answers were intentional or due to the fact that he had carried her nearly half the length of the docks.

"I'm sorry I broke the contract." She tightened her arms around his neck, thinking to make his task easier.

"You could have been killed."

"I know."

He grunted.

"It was a stupid thing to do," she added, and then a shiver ran through her.

"You're cold." He halted his footsteps. "Let me give you my jacket." He moved to set her down but Lydia simply clung to him tighter.

"Just hold me. I was so stupid today. I nearly got you killed."

"No." Agony sounded in his voice. "You nearly got *you* killed. Don't ever do that again." The look on his face was bleak. "I couldn't live... God, Lydia, I couldn't live without you."

His arms tightened and he buried his face in her hair.

"Arthur was a traitor Lydia." He sounded pained, wounded. "*My brother* was in Farley's employ. His actions cost the lives of five other men. Possibly more."

Lydia squeezed him tighter. It was the only thing she could do to hold this proud man together.

"I wanted him to be innocent. I was so sure..."

"You did everything you could. You were the best brother he could have asked for." And then she pulled away to stare at him. "You brought Blackheart along with you to save me." Her statement was really a question.

Jeremy resumed walking and she waited patiently for his answer.

"I blamed him and Lucas. I made Lucas the enemy simply because I didn't want to believe it could be true. But Arthur's name was among those who'd been paid off."

"He didn't want to work for Farley," Lydia said. "He simply ran out of choices." She went on to tell him all that she'd learned from Farley and Buck. About how they'd trapped him with his debts and then how, after the ambush, Arthur refused to do their bidding again.

Jeremy didn't say anything, he simply kept marching along the walk as he listened to her.

"So you know, then." He finally said.

"There wasn't anything you could do," she pressed. He had to know this in his heart.

"I could have helped him with those debts. I could have paid them off myself."

"And then what? Knowing Arthur, he likely would have racked up new ones quicker than he did the first."

"I should have been able to help him." His voice caught, and in the moonlight, Lydia watched as a single tear rolled down his cheek. She caught it with her thumb and pressed a soft kiss against his jaw.

And Jeremy just kept walking. He might have truly been prepared to carry her all the way to Mayfair had his driver not been watching for him. He finally dipped her feet to the ground as the familiar coach slowed to a stop beside them.

"Excellent to see you safe and sound, My Lady." The driver spoke from his box while a manservant pulled down the step. "To Cork Street, My Lord?"

"Yes," Jeremy answered.

The last time she and Jeremy had ridden in this carriage had been only one night before. So much had changed in the matter of a single day.

Lydia settled onto the bench and Jeremy climbed in behind her, but then she moved naturally into his arms as the carriage jerked into motion.

"Did you mean it?" he asked in a gravelly voice.

"Of course." There was no need to question his meaning. He'd received the letter. "I never stopped loving you, and I never will."

She'd always heard it was foolish to express her feelings so easily, but she was learning that life was too tenuous to play games.

"I don't deserve you." He squeezed her against him. "I never stopped loving you either. I just didn't know how... I couldn't ask you—"

"You did what you had to, and I love you more now than I did before. I'm only sorry you've had to deal with this alone."

"But I hurt you."

"You thought you were protecting me." She now understood why he'd pushed her away. It reminded her of how Ollie had tried to convince her to turn away when she'd found him in the Warehouse yard. "Everything happens for a reason. Because of you, there's no way of knowing how many lives will be saved. You are a hero."

Jeremy shook his head, making a scoffing sound.

"Oh, no." He needed to see what others saw. "You may have gone into this thinking only to clear Arthur's name but you've come out having accomplished an incredible feat. No one else was willing to take them on until you did."

"You almost have me believing that. I don't deserve you, Lydia."

"Oh, but you do." They were meant for one another in every way. The sooner he accepted this the sooner the two of them could go on with their lives—together.

Jeremy buried his face in her hair. "Marry me?"

The question wasn't at all what she'd been expecting just then, and these were not at all the circumstances in which she'd imagined he would ask but...

This was Jeremy.

"You aren't just asking this because my brother has returned to town?"

He released her and shuffled through his pockets. When he located what he was looking for, he dangled a small velvet pouch in front of her. She'd seen such a pouch recently, when Blackheart had purchased some jewelry for his new duchess.

Lydia held her breath while Jeremy untied the drawstring and reached inside.

"I bought this yesterday. Shortly after the completion of the sale." Lydia gasped when she caught sight of a sparkling diamond set in a circle of gold clutched between his thumb and finger. It reflected every single star that twinkled through the window. "I meant to propose to you today at the warehouse. But then everything went crazy. I know this isn't very romantic or at all proper, but—"

Lydia cut him off by pressing her mouth to his. When their lips parted on a sigh, she opened her eyes and met his gaze. "You're all I've ever wanted. Of course I'll marry you."

EPILOGUE

*J*eremy entered the drawing room where the Duke of Blackheart stood with his back to him, staring out the window. Simon Cockfield had been one of his closest friends for most of his life. They had both been their fathers' heirs—and became the heads of their family at very young ages. But before that, they'd spent summers together pretending to be pirates, running like banshee's back and forth between their fathers' lands. They had been confidants. Schoolmates. And then as adults, they'd offered one another support.

As Blackheart had today, showing up in Jeremy's time of need, bringing additional manpower. And he had not poured salt into his wound knowing the truth now, about Arthur.

Jeremy ran a hand through his hair. "I need to thank you."

Blackheart turned his head, meeting Jeremy's gaze. "You'd have done the same for me."

But Jeremy was shaking his head. "Not this year. I've been—"

"He was your brother. You did what you needed to do." The duke's eyes spoke volumes. "I'd have done the same... if the situations had been reversed."

That elephant that had been sitting on Jeremy's chest shifted, giving him some relief. Because Blackheart would not speak platitudes to him.

"How is Lucas?" Jeremy asked. Lucas had been Arthur's commander. It had been men in Arthur's unit who had been killed.

If anyone had a right to be angry, it was Lucas.

"Lucas... is letting go. With Naomi at his side, and baby Amelia, he simply wants to put it behind them. They are in Kent now but would welcome a visit, I'm sure."

Jeremy would make amends then. But for now...

He cleared his throat. "There is another discussion I need to have with you."

Upon these words, the corner of Blackheart's mouth tilted up ever so slightly. "A discussion about my sister."

"Yes." Lydia. The promise he'd nearly lost. "I've asked her to marry me, and she has agreed."

"Of course, she has."

"I want you to know that I love her. And I'll spend what remains of my life doing all that I can to make her happy."

Was Blackheart's exhale an expression of relief? "Excellent."

"I still can't imagine what you were thinking, allowing her to be in London on her own... starting up orphanages, running about the docks." Jeremy laughed softly. "Although I suppose I ought to thank you."

Blackheart lifted one brow. "Do you really think I did not know what my sister was up to?"

"You knew?"

Blackheart stilled. "You needed her. And she was quietly dying inside after you broke things off. One word in Baxter's ear was all it took."

"Ah." Of course, Blackheart had known. And Baxter as well. Jeremy shook his head. "Well." He could not be angry, even though he thought he ought to be. But having Lydia's promise to marry him and having thoroughly kissed her less than a quarter of an hour ago, he could only grin. "It worked. Although now I've got an orphanage to get up and running."

"Speaking of my sister…" Blackheart's brows rose.

"She'll be down momentarily. I wanted to speak with you first. I take it we have your blessing then?"

His friend shifted him a suspicious glance. "Tell me that a special license is not necessary."

"No," Jeremy said. Although… just barely.

"Then you have my blessing."

"We'll want to have the banns read starting this Sunday. I've already waited too long…" And he meant it. He'd waited his lifetime for Lydia. "But I won't take her dowry."

At this, Blackheart laughed. "Good thing, as she's spent most of it on that damn warehouse."

Jeremy shook his head.

"But I've a portion we'll put into trust. We'll discuss

contracts later," Blackheart added, just as the door crept open slowly.

Having bathed, Lydia had changed into an old gown of his mother's. And she still managed to steal his breath with her beauty.

Lydia peered inside, her eyes flicking between the two of them questioningly . "All is well?"

She met Jeremy's gaze, and he smiled reassuringly. "I believe so. Simon?"

Blackheart glared at Jeremy at the use of his Christian name, but then turned to Lydia and held out a hand. "Come here, you little fool. You could have been killed."

Lydia all but flew into her brother's arms. "I know. I'm so sorry."

Blackheart was not a man known for showing his emotions, and Jeremy was surprised to see something that resembled both love and pain flicker across the man's face.

"I'm only grateful you are safe." Blackheart pressed his jaw against the top of her head and then set her away from him. "But you are never—absolutely never—to go down to the docks alone again. If you do, I will throttle you. And if I'm not there, Tempest will do the honors. Do you understand?"

A mysterious smile tugged at her lips. "I do," she agreed, far too easily.

"I mean it." Blackheart was almost wholly his ducal self again.

"As do I," Jeremy added.

Lydia squeezed her brother's hand and then moved away from him, crossing to Jeremy, who couldn't help but reach out and draw her close. But he addressed her brother. "I'll send notices of our engagement to the papers first thing tomorrow." Then he stared down into his fiancée's eyes. "And to St. George's."

Lydia beamed up at him.

"We can talk more tomorrow." Blackheart moved to go. "My duchess will be wondering where I've run off to. Do you have a coat?" As was only proper, he'd come to take Lydia home with him.

Lydia, of course, wasn't so easily managed by her brother. Even if he was Blackheart.

"I need to tell Ollie goodnight, and Lady Tempest asked me to tell her goodbye as well. I've no doubt Lord Tempest can bring me home shortly in his carriage." And before Blackheart could object, she asked, "What is going to happen to Buck?"

"Ah." Blackheart rubbed his chin. "I've had the boy taken to Heart Place for now. Lost most of his hand."

"You've taken him to Heart Place?" Lydia looked as shocked by her brother's admission as Jeremy was.

"He risks infection, but if he pulls through..." Blackheart lifted his chin. "He was terrified of dying in Newgate, and as I'm not certain he's as hardened as he pretends to be. If he lives, I'll see what I can do to help him."

Lydia's eyes filled with tears. Jeremy knew those tears. They were the same ones he'd seen in her eyes when he'd agreed to bring Ollie back to Cork Street.

Even so... "I'd be wary of him."

"I think it's wonderful." Lydia smiled. "But you must

be exhausted. Go home to your duchess, brother, and I'll return to Heart Place shortly."

Blackheart glanced over at the clock on the mantel. "Within the hour."

Lydia nodded. She had already pushed him farther than Jeremy would have imagined he'd allow.

Jeremy could hardly wait to have her in his home every night—in his life. He almost wished he'd insisted on that special license after all.

Leaving Lydia in the drawing room, Jeremy walked Blackheart to the door. He reached out. "Thank you again."

Blackheart grasped Jeremy's hand and squeezed it almost painfully. "If you ever hurt her again, I'll kill you."

"If I ever hurt her again, I'll deserve it."

LYDIA SAT ON THE SETTEE, waiting for Jeremy to return, smiling when she saw a replacement vase sitting on the table behind it.

"My clever girl," he said from the door.

In answer, she lifted her arms, thrilled as he slowly crossed the room, not taking his gaze off her for a moment.

"Ollie is already sleeping," he said, lowering himself beside her.

"I know."

"And my mother is as well." He wound his arms around her.

"I know." Lydia burrowed into him. "I just needed to

be alone with you a little longer. It's going to feel like forever before all the banns have been read."

Lydia couldn't help but slide her gaze to the vase on the table behind them. "It is only a replica?"

"It is." But he wasn't looking at the vase. He was staring at her, his eyes looking darker than normal, his pupils dilated. His lashes dropped when his gaze flicked to her mouth.

"Was it expensive?" Lydia asked, licking her lips.

"It's worthless. Almost a disgrace to display it in my home." He was stroking her lips with his thumb now, and she could see the pulse at the base of his neck racing.

Almost as fast as hers was.

"In that case…"

Lydia turned and straddled him the same as she had before.

"You're dangerous. Do you know that?"

Lydia simply nodded. "I love you Jeremy."

"I love you, Lydia."

Not quite ten minutes later, the new vase lay shattered on the floor.

* The End *

Want more of Lydia and Jeremy?
Grab your copy of the Earl of Tempest
BONUS Epilogue here!
https://BookHip.com/ZWDMTQ

Thank you for reading Jeremy and Lydia's story.
If you haven't read *Ruined*,

Lord Lucas and Arthur's widow's story,
you can read it here:
https://books2read.com/AnnabelleAnders-Ruined

The Earl of Tempest, in addition to being included in the Wicked Earls Club, is part of my Regency Cocky Gents Series.

MORE WICKED EARLS!

Turn the page to read chapter one of
EARL OF KENDAL,
the next book in the Wicked Earl's Club,
by *Madeline Martin.*
(Release Date: Jan. 19, 2021)

EARL OF KENDAL

BY MADELINE MARTIN

*L*ondon, England
March 1822

ADOLPHUS MERRICK, the third Earl of Kendal, had been accused many times in his life of being unfeeling. It was a claim he did not refute. Why would he when it so often played to his benefit?

He slid a cool glance toward his left where his sister, Lady Marguerite Merrick, stood in men's attire. She had gone without the concealment of the mask she usually wore when overseeing Mercy's Door, the gaming hell they owned together. After all, she was well acquainted with Lord Gullsville. He was one of the few members of the ton who knew her true identity.

It was through his generosity that she had been spared. But Lord Gullsville didn't regard her with equal fondness at present. He flicked a nervous glance in her direction. "She doesn't have to be here, does she?"

Irritation squeezed at Kendal's gut as he surmised at that moment what the other man wanted.

Money.

Again.

"She's as much of a part of this operation as I am," Kendal replied dryly. "As you well know."

Gullsville ran a hand over his cropped, silver hair.

"You've requested an audience with me." Kendal leaned back in his seat, putting himself at ease when the other man was so clearly in discomfort. "Why?"

"Fox's Den," Gullsville muttered the name of Kendal's rival gaming hell with a fitting level of shame.

"I beg your pardon?" Kendal asked, despite having heard perfectly well the first time.

Gullsville lifted his head in agitation. The tip of his straight nose was threaded with spidery veins, and his eyes were perpetually bloodshot. A habitual drinker. One who had not honored his family properly after his wife had passed.

If he hadn't saved Marguerite...

"Fox's Den," Lord Gullsville repeated with vehemence.

Why was it that sods in trouble became angry at the ones there to help them out?

Marguerite cast Kendal a sympathetic shake of her head. She always did have a soft spot for the older man.

Still, Kendal was loathe to open his safe to the man. Especially after the Earl of Gullsville had burned through his own annual income and an additional two thousand pounds Kendal had graciously loaned him.

"How much do you owe this time?" Kendal drawled out.

In response, Gullsville exhaled heavily. A wash of his sour breath swept over the short distance of the desk.

Kendal kept his face impassive, but his stomach twisted—more with dread than at offense at the odor.

Lord Gullsville had never hesitated to speak a number before. Whatever the man had to say would not be good.

Gullsville pressed his lips shut, opening them as he took a breath in preparation to speak. "Th...three..."

Kendal gritted his teeth. "Three hundred?" He kept his voice intentionally bland to conceal his growing aggravation.

The man winced, evidently aware of how abysmal his situation was due to his vice.

Kendal had a reputation for being unfeeling, yes, but in truth, he was not. In fact, he cared too much.

He could not airily push aside his loyalty to the man who had saved Marguerite when Kendal had nowhere else to turn.

Nor could he nudge away the knowledge that Gullsville had a son who would someday inherit the earldom—however tattered it might be—and a married daughter and a younger unwed daughter who had yet to set her heart on a beau. The latter was a lovely thing, one with enough interest to choose any husband she wanted. And unfortunately, one who appeared to be in no hurry to stop spending her father's dwindling funds and settle down.

No, he couldn't leave the man destitute.

"Three hundred?" Kendal repeated for confirmation as he pushed up to his feet. "This is the last time, Gullsville."

"Three thousand." Lord Gullsville expelled the appalling number from his chest in a puffed exhale.

Kendal froze. Marguerite's eyes shot to his, conveying the same horror that was now crystalizing like ice in his veins.

"You are aware we are not a bank?" Kendal regarded the man.

"It is a considerable sum, yes, I know," Gullsville rushed. "I was down. I didn't want to come to you again and thought I could win. I was so close, but the other man had an ace. An ace." He balled his hand into a fist. "If it had been any other card, any other..." His voice trailed off as he watched Kendal.

Gullsville gave a hard swallow. "You aren't going to help me, are you?"

"You ask too much," Marguerite said.

He swung his attention toward her and his expression crumpled with desperation. "My son must have something left to inherit. And my Sophia is still unwed. You wouldn't have them to suffer the faults of their wretched father, would you?"

Marguerite looked away. A certain indicator her resolve was cracking.

"I saved you." Gullsville's words were whispered, but they rang out in the room like a gunshot.

"Don't." Kendal was in front of the older man in a flash.

Marguerite turned her head more firmly away. No longer the strong, confident figure she'd become, but once more the damaged girl.

But then, everyone had their Achilles' heel, didn't they?

The earl knew both of theirs, and he was digging into those tender wounds with meat hooks.

Gullsville ignored Kendal, his gaze fixed pointedly on Marguerite. "I saved you when you would have otherwise been ruined. You owe this to me."

Kendal blocked the older man's view of Marguerite. "Gullsville, I warn you—"

"If it weren't for me, your sister would be just as tarnished as your mother." Gullsville curled his lip. "Just another whore."

Kendal's fist shot out before he could even think to stop it. Not that he would have.

His knuckles connected with Gullsville's jaw with an intensity that made the older man's head jerk upright. His lashes didn't so much as flutter as he collapsed gracelessly to the floor.

Silence filled the small room. Kendal put his back to the earl and regarded his sister. Her eyes, a deep brown that was nearly black, so like his own—so like their mother's—were wide with a vulnerability he hadn't seen in years.

It made the place inside him that needed to protect, that wound that would never fully heal, split open. He wanted to tell her all would be well. And he wanted to say it without lying.

"Are you all right?" he asked tentatively.

Her pointed chin notched, and her eyes flashed with defiance. "Of course, I am." She withdrew a black mask from her jacket pocket. The thing fit her from forehead to chin and obscured all of the beauty she'd inherited from their mother. Which was exactly what Marguerite wanted.

The disguise had left their patrons talking for years about Marcus, the name Marguerite had adopted, with conjecture and wild assumptions. It was rumored Marcus was really a duke determined to protect his identity. Or he was a victim of a terrible fire that had burned most of his body and left him horribly disfigured.

On and on the speculation went, growing more preposterous as time carried on. Yet no one assumed the most amazing truth of all: Marcus was Marguerite, a woman who shunned society and the ton's hypocrites. A woman who once resigned herself to life in the country before fighting for a chance to come back and thrive in London the only way she could bear.

She gave a wounded look to where Gullsville lay on the carpet. "I'll see to it that he's taken care of. You've a ball to attend, do you not?"

Kendal hesitated, hating to leave Marguerite to handle the situation. Not that she wasn't capable. God knew she was.

But he knew better than to argue. All the protests wouldn't keep Marguerite from nudging him out the door and to the ball, where he would most likely be in attendance with Gullsville's son and youngest daughter.

~

LADY SOPHIA STOPFORD, the youngest child of the Earl of Gullsville, had always loved a ball. Not only for the gowns, though they were indeed lovely, or even for the eligible men who kept her dancing through the night. No, it was the effervescent energy quivering in the room, as though the air alone was enough to make the bubbles tickle up the sides of delicate glassware.

Tonight, however, even the anticipation could scarcely elevate her spirits.

"I say, Sophia, are you even listening?"

She blinked and regarded Henry, Viscount Southby, her older brother, who strode at her side up the path to Bursbury Manor, where her aunt was hosting a ball for the coming out of her youngest daughter, Lady Eugenia.

Sophia shook her head. "I'm sorry, I—" She stopped herself from making an excuse. "I was woolgathering. Do forgive me, dear brother."

He tilted his head, a concerned look crossing his handsome face. They had all inherited the same gentle appearance. But while Sophia and their eldest sister, Cecelia, had delicate features, Henry's were elegantly sculpted, and his eyes were kind.

Those eyes were now scrutinizing her with tender perception. "You've been put out since your conversation with Father earlier."

Sophia looked away to discourage him from reading

her like a broadsheet. Her conversation with their father had indeed not gone well. Not only did he feel it was time for her to wed, but he had also found the man she ought to marry.

Mr. Mongerton, the owner of a gaming hell—the Fox Hole—or something equally as crass. An associate, Father had called him. As if actual business transpired between them. Not that she was allowed to argue. She was the second daughter, as he so bluntly stated.

And while Sophia could not argue her birth order, she did not agree that it relegated her to a position where she ought to wed a man over twice her own age.

This was not how it was all supposed to go. She hadn't put off marriage for so long so that she could be wed to an associate of her father's. She'd done it so she could have the full experience of the joy of youth before being tethered into matrimony. Her vow to live her life to the fullest had not been in vain, even if her father had no appreciation for such matters.

And while she understood Father's impatience, did he really have to select someone as ghastly as Mr. Mongerton?

The gaming hell owner had made his interest in her known on more than one occasion with beady and lascivious glances her way. The very idea of the man made her flesh crawl with distaste.

Sophia rose on her tiptoes with feigned excitement to see who was in the entryway and mask her shudder of revulsion. "Did you see if Lord Heaton has arrived yet?"

"Is Lord Heaton the one to have finally captured your heart, little sister?" Henry kept his voice low. He always was mindful of her feelings. It was one of the many things she adored about him.

"You know he is not," she hissed in a happy whisper. "Though he dances beautifully, don't you think?"

"I was going to say exactly that very thing about him myself," Henry said with a smile and offered Sophia his arm as they approached the bright entryway to the ballroom in preparation of being announced.

Sophia couldn't help but laugh as she accepted his arm.

"Perhaps it might be better if you refrain from dancing as much this evening." Henry offered her an apologetic smile. "In light of our cousin's coming out."

Heat touched Sophia's cheeks, but she understood his implication. It was a rare night when Sophia's dance card had any space on it for another suitor. Tonight, was for Eugenia to shine. Which Sophia had already taken into consideration.

"I'm wearing my slippers without a heel," she admitted. "On account of my twisted ankle."

Henry winked at her in appreciation of her feigned injury.

The caller announced them, and Eugenia sailed toward them with a smile beaming on her red lips. Sophia had been at the modiste with her cousin when her coming out gown was designed, and it was stunning. Pale blue fabric with deeper blue rosettes crafted in silk over the full skirt and matching slippers. Her red hair had been twisted into an elaborate arrangement with silver ribbons and her freshly crimped curls gleamed in the candlelight.

The fashion was more elaborate than Sophia's own light brown tresses, which had been left intentionally simple. A woman's coming out was her crowning achievement, and Sophia would do nothing to take that away from her cousin and dearest friend.

"Isn't it grand?" Eugenia squealed and surveyed the ballroom. Garlands of roses were resplendent in the large room, all matching colors to her attire. The wooden floor had been polished to a high shine, and candles glittered in mirrored sconces, making the room glow with golden light.

Eugenia's elder sister caught Sophia's eye and offered a delicate wave. Penelope, the Countess of Oakhurst, generally did not attend balls now that she was wed to the Earl of Oakhurst, but she was not only in attendance but also appeared to be enjoying herself.

"The grandest." Sophia embraced her cousin. "I'm so very happy for you."

Eugenia grabbed her hand. "Come, let's find eligible men to dance with." She bit her lip, her eyes dancing with mirth. "And perhaps one to marry."

"I find myself in need of some brandy." Henry offered a bow, gave Eugenia a compliment on her ribbons or something of the like, and wandered swiftly away from the conversation of suitors and marriage.

Typical man.

"Ah, Sophia, there you are, dearest." Lady Bursbury swept to Sophia's side. "Might I steal your cousin away for a moment, Eugenia?"

At that moment, Lord Heaton arrived, and a mischievous sparkle lit Eugenia's blue eyes. "Be sure to find me when you're done," she said.

Lady Bursbury watched her walk away, a slight twist to her mouth. "She'll be a tough one to keep from marrying too quickly."

"I thought you wanted everyone married off, Aunt Nancy," Sophia said it playfully.

The little laugh Lady Bursbury gave told her she took Sophia's words exactly that way. "Yes, but happily, my dear." She leaned toward Sophia and lowered her voice. "Which is why I've come to speak to you." The concern in her sharp blue eyes was unmistakable.

She knew.

"I take it my father has spoken to you?" Sophia surmised.

Her aunt sighed. "I asked him to give me a chance to find you someone different. Someone more appropriate. He seems rather set on his decision. However..." She lifted one auburn brow triumphantly. "I can be very persuasive."

Sophia grinned. Lady Bursbury could be very persuasive indeed, especially when it came to matchmaking, of which she was quite adept. Even Cecelia hadn't been able to avoid their aunt's schemes.

"I think you've met most of the men of the ton already." Lady Bursbury tapped her fan to her palm repeatedly as her gaze skimmed the room. "I've had someone in mind for you for quite a while but have been waiting until just the right moment."

Excitement lit within Sophia. Hope.

Her aunt gave up searching the room and whispered, "Lord Kendal."

Sophia held herself upright to keep from wilting at the declaration.

She must not have been very convincing, as Lady Bursbury gave a little pout. "What is it? Have you decided against him already?"

"Well, he's a far cry better than Mr. Mongerton, but all he ever does is talk amongst the men and he never bothers to dance. He's so very..." Sophia glanced around them as she spoke to confirm he was not nearby. "Bor—"

She'd been on the tip of saying "boring" when her eyes locked with the dark gaze of a tall, lean man just behind them.

Lord Kendal.

"Oh, don't be ridiculous," Lady Bursbury said, oblivious of his proximity. "He's hardly boring."

He gave Sophia a small tight smile, which she tried to return as best she could.

"I'll go find him now and speak to him." Lady Bursbury slapped her fan in her palm one final time with determination.

Lord Kendal gave a small bow and backed away from them, disappearing into the crush of people. This time Sophia didn't bother to protest. There was no point when it was obvious there was no discouraging Aunt Nancy.

Not that any of it would do any good, regardless. Sophia knew her father well enough to be keenly aware he would not be swayed into changing his mind.

Short of fleeing England, there would be nothing for

it but to marry Mongerton. And while fleeing England did hold great appeal, what was she to do if she did leave? She would require lodging, money, a way to generate an income.

What she needed was a miracle. Or an excellent idea.

GRAB YOUR COPY AT: Books2Read:
https://books2read.com/EarlOfKendal

REGENCY COCKY GENTS

Each book can be read as a stand alone but is connected as a series.

Book 1: Cocky Earl

The Earl of Westerley and the American Whiskey King's daughter.

Book 2: Cocky Baron

Baron Chaswick and Lady Bethany (Westerleys' sister)

Book 3: Cocky Mister

Mr. Stone Spencer and Lady Tabetha (Westerley's sister)

Book 3.5 Mayfair Maiden

Mr. Peter Spencer and Lady Starling

Book 4: Cocky Viscount

The Viscount Manningham-Tissinton and Lady Felicity

Book 5: Cocky Marquess

The Marquess of Greystone's story

Book 6: Cocky Butler

The Duke of Blackheart's story.

Ruined

Blackheart's younger brother (Lord Lucas) and Naomi

Earl of Tempest

Blackheart's sister (Lydia) and Lord Tempest

ABOUT ANNABELLE ANDERS

Married to the same man for over 25 years, I am a mother to three children and two Miniature Wiener dogs.

After owning a business and experiencing considerable success, my husband and I got caught in the financial crisis and lost everything in 2008; our business, our home, even our car.

At this point, I put my B.A. in Poly Sci to use and took work as a waitress and bartender (Insert irony). Unwilling to give up on a professional life, I simultaneously went back to college and obtained a degree in Energy Management.

And then the energy market dropped off.

And then my dog died.

I can only be grateful for this series of unfortunate events, for, with nothing to lose and completely demoralized, I sat down and began to write the romance novels which had until then, existed only my imagination. After publishing over thirty novels now, with one having been nominated for RWA's Distinguished ™RITA Award in 2019, I am happy to tell you that I have finally found my place in life.

Thank you so much for being a part of my journey!

To find out more about my books, and also to download a free novella, get all the info at my website!
www.annabelleanders.com

facebook.com/Annabelle.Anders1
instagram.com/annabelle.anders